STAR WARS

REBEL ✪ FORCE

HOSTAGE

BY ALEX WHEELER

LUCAS BOOKS

SCHOLASTIC INC.

New York Toronto London Auckland Sydney Mexico City New Delhi Hong Kong Buenos Aires

www.starwars.com
www.scholastic.com

ISBN-13: 978-0-545-11218-5
ISBN-10: 0-545-11218-4

12 11 10 9 8 7 6 5 4 3 2 1   9 10 11 12 13 14/0

Designed by Rick DeMonico
Cover illustrations by Randy Martinez
Printed in the U.S.A.
First printing, January 2009

ay never came to the swamp. The dank air, thick with swirling fumes, shrouded the land in eternal fog. The distant sun emitted only a dim glow, turning the sky a sallow green that matched his skin. Until, all too soon, night fell once again.

He, who had devoted his life to the light, now lived in darkness. It seemed the universe liked a good joke.

And so he laughed.

"Too dark to see my breakfast, it is," he chortled, stirring some rootleaf and gnarltree bark into the bowl of butcherbug stew. He wrinkled his nose at the foul stench. "Perhaps lucky, I am, hmm."

He spoke to himself often here. Another joke: That he, who had taken such joy in others, was alone. Alone in an empty swamp; alone on an empty planet.

Alone, yet not alone: He still had the Force.

It was a Padawan's first lesson: Learn to trust your senses — and learn to reach beyond them. He did not need light to see.

Nor did he need to see the faces of his allies to know they were there.

"Waiting for you, I have been," he said softly, hunched over the makeshift stove. His stew bubbled over the flame. Another Padawan lesson: When the time comes to eat, *eat*. Food runs out. So does time.

His modest hut had been empty for a long time. For many years, his shuffling footsteps had been the only ones to cross the threshhold; his halting wheeze had been the only breath to mist across the still air.

He was alone still — and yet, not alone.

"I have failed, Master," the voice said.

He shook his head. "Failed, we all have," he said. "Succeed, we all may. Undetermined, the future is." He had seen the future in his dreams. Cloudy visions of blood and fire, terror mixed with hope, death with awakening.

"I have much to tell you," the voice said urgently.

He rummaged through a pile of junk, pulling out a misshapen spoon. He had crafted it himself from a fallen gnarltree branch. "Patience, Obi-Wan," he said, finally turning to face the spirit of the fallen Jedi. "Talk, we will, hmm, yes. But first, eat, I must."

As Obi-Wan Kenobi's shimmering figure looked on, casting a soft glow of light around the dark cave, the great

Jedi Master Yoda shuffled over to a narrow wooden table. He lowered his frail, stooped body onto a wobbly stool.

And he ate his breakfast.

"He's powerful, Master Yoda," Obi-Wan said. "I can sense it within him. Young, but —"

"Young, yes." Yoda nodded. "And old, too. Yes, yes. Too old?" Never had a Jedi begun his training as an adult. Brought to the Jedi Temple as infants, they grew up knowing nothing but the Jedi way. In Yoda's long memory, only one exception had been made on this front. One Padawan so promising that it seemed foolish not to train him, though he was already nine years old, with memories of a different world and attachments to a different life.

The Jedi Council had allowed the training to proceed, though they'd had their doubts. Rather than trusting his judgment, Yoda had put his trust in Qui-Gon Jinn — and Anakin Skywalker.

Yes, they had all failed, one way or another.

"He's impatient," Obi-Wan admitted. His face was webbed by deep creases, his eyes underlined with dark hollows. Death had not relieved him of the burdens he carried. "And stubborn. "

"Remind me, that does, of another young Jedi."

Obi-Wan frowned. "*No.* The boy is nothing like his father."

"Not Anakin," Yoda said mildly. "You." He smiled, remembering the brash young man who, from the start, had wielded his lightsaber like it was a part of him.

"The boy must be trained, but he is impulsive," Obi-Wan said. "Courageous, bright, loyal, yes — and yet, quick to anger, impatient. Perhaps too willing to choose the easy path."

"Human, he is," Yoda pointed out. "Flawed, all living beings are."

"He has greatness in him," Obi-Wan said. "Of that I am sure. But as to what form the greatness will take . . ." He hung his head. "I was sure about Anakin, too. Once."

"Responsibility, we must all take," Yoda said firmly. "You, for your choice. Me, for mine. *Anakin* — only Anakin — for his."

Obi-Wan paused, the guilt plain on his face. Yoda knew he blamed himself. For Anakin, for Darth Vader . . . for all that followed.

"We need Luke," Obi-Wan said. "But if we proceed too quickly . . . if we make the wrong choices . . ." He sighed. "I sense great power in him, perhaps greater even than Anakin's."

"Search inside yourself," Yoda said. "Know the answer, you do."

"He is too old for us to shape," Obi-Wan said slowly, as if sifting through his thoughts as he spoke. "He is nei-ther Padawan nor Master. He has grown into his own person, without our help or interference — now we must give him the space to grow into his own man." Obi-Wan sighed, gazing out at the murky bog, then up at the stars. "He will be tested — I cannot save him from that. He *must* be tested. Perhaps this was our mistake with Anakin. Not that we found him too late, but that we put too much upon him too soon. We burdened him with power he could not control, with responsibility he could not bear. This time, we must be cautious — let Luke become the man he needs to be. And hope that this is the man

we need him to be."

Yoda nodded. This was the same judgment he had reached. "Ready, he is not," Yoda said. "Patient we must be."

They could not let fear of Luke's future prevent them from training the boy. But they could equally not let their own eagerness for a champion fool them into seeing something that wasn't there.

And, of course, Luke was not their only hope.

There was another.

CHAPTER TWO

Princess Leia Organa felt a prickly tingle run up her spine — someone was watching her.

She didn't turn around. "See anything that interests you?" She kept her eyes focused on the data-pad in her lap, but the screen might as well have been blank. She hadn't been able to concentrate for hours. The closer they got to their destination, the faster her thoughts seemed to swim away from her.

"Not a thing, princess." Normally, Han Solo's sarcastic drawl made her want to put her fist through a bulkhead. But at a moment like this, Han's voice — his presence — was almost a comfort.

Almost.

"Well?" she snapped. "What is it?"

"You asked me to let you know when we dropped out of hyperspace," he reminded her. "This is me, letting you know."

Leia suppressed a shudder. Or, at least, she tried to.

She heard Han take a step into the cabin. Then another. "Leia . . ."

"I'll join you in the cockpit in a few minutes," she said coolly, keeping her back to him and her posture rigid. "I want to watch the approach."

"It'll be a rough one."

"I think I can handle it."

"You *think* you can handle anything," Han countered. "That's the problem."

"No, the problem is *you* trying to tell me what I can and can't do." The banter was making her feel more normal than she had all day. *Guess being trapped in space with a nerf-herding laserbrain has its advantages,* she thought.

"Maybe you forget, Your Highnessness, but I'm captain of this bird. That means I say what *everyone* can and can't do."

"And *I* say I'll be joining you in the cockpit in a few minutes," she said, durasteel in her voice.

She heard his footsteps retreat toward the door. "You know, you don't have to do this."

Leia brushed a hand across her cheek, enraged to find it dotted with moisture. She shut her eyes and took a deep, shaky breath. Then she finally faced him. "Yes," she said, in a low, dangerous voice. "I do."

"Suit yourself, princess." He snorted. "You always do."

She waited until he was gone, then wrapped her arms across her chest, encasing herself in a tight hug. "Pull yourself together," she murmured. "It's just another landing."

And it would be. Landing on Delaya would be total routine — but to get there, they would have to make it through a dangerous storm of debris. Millions of whirling meteors, some no larger than her fist, others several times more massive than the *Millennium Falcon*. A collision could prove fatal.

Except it wasn't *debris*, Leia thought. It wasn't *trash*.

It was all that remained of the planet Alderaan. What had been a thriving planet, home to two billion people, was now nothing more than a few rocks spiraling through the emptiness of space.

Leia set the datapad beside her on the bunk. She twisted her hair back into two long braids and wrapped them around her head. Then she stood.

She wasn't ready — but the moment had arrived, ready or not.

It was time to go home.

Han muttered a silent curse as Leia climbed into the cockpit. With the densest debris field this side of the galaxy to navigate, the last thing he needed was a distraction. Especially the worrying-about-Leia kind of distraction.

He wasn't supposed to have to worry about anyone but himself. And now, all of a sudden, he was mixed up in this ridiculous Rebel Alliance business, saddled with a handful of trouble-making passengers and their annoying droids.

In addition to the princess, there was Luke Skywalker, who fancied himself some kind of Jedi warrior — and who was lucky he hadn't sliced off an arm with that lightsaber of his. Yet. There was Tobin Elad, the resistance fighter they'd picked up on the way to Muunilinst — an impressive pilot, an even more impressive fighter, a quick thinker, no friend to the Empire . . . Han might even have enjoyed having him around. *Might* — if the princess hadn't made it so painfully clear that she found Elad superior in every way that counted. He could do nothing wrong. While Han, as far as Leia was concerned, could do nothing right.

Fine with me, he thought. It was time to start treating this like any other job. He would drop them on Delaya, as promised — but that would be the end of it. He had a life of his own, after all. People to scam, places to go, Hutts to repay.

"Entering the Alderaan system." Han cut the thrusters to reduce speed. "Delaya's on the other side of the debris field. No way around but straight through." The storm of whirling rock loomed in the viewscreen. Delaya lay just beyond. Once it had been Alderaan's sister planet.

Now it was an only child.

Leia's face paled. Luke's jaw tightened. Chewbacca let loose a mournful howl.

Han couldn't blame him. You could almost feel it pressing in around you: *death*. Two billion lives, gone up in a ball of flame. For a single, horrifying moment, he imagined their faces — pale, terrified, *dead* — flattening themselves against the cockpit window.

I feel a great disturbance in the Force, as if millions of voices suddenly cried out in terror and were suddenly silenced, the old man had said. Like he could sense it happening.

Han shook it off. *You're starting to sound like Luke*, he warned himself. *You're not sensing anything but a rough landing. And if you don't start focusing on these rocks, there might not be a landing at all.*

"Better strap in," he warned his passengers. As he spoke, the ship lurched as a large rock slammed into the starboard deflector shield. Caught off guard, Leia toppled forward. Han caught her just before she crashed into an instrument panel. "You okay?" he said, trying to steady her.

She ripped her arm away. "I'll be *okay* when we land this thing," she snapped. "How about you try focusing on that."

"Yes, ma'am," he said sarcastically. "But only because you asked so nicely." She had some nerve, giving him orders on the bridge of *his* ship. Who did she think she —

"Whoa!" Han swore, jerking the *Falcon* sharply to the port side, moments before crashing into a ship-sized asteroid. "Focus. Right. Good plan."

Chewbacca growled at the viewscreen.

"I see it, buddy," Han said, steering the ship around another asteroid. They were hurtling toward him from all sides now. He eased the *Falcon* through the gaps, diving and weaving to avoid the larger rocks. The smaller ones battered the shields. The ship shook and shuddered, the controls vibrating in his grip. Behind him, somewhere in the bowels of the ship, there was a soft hissing noise, then a loud bang. A moment later, the acrid scent of smoke trickled into the cockpit. "Chewie, the aft deflector must have taken a hit. Get back there and check it out!"

The Wookiee was already in motion. Luke's astromech droid followed closely on his heels.

"Captain, may I recommend that you avoid crashing into anything else?" the protocol droid C-3PO suggested.

"May I recommend you take a long walk through a short airlock?" Han growled, swerving to starboard and then sharply to port, as another flood of debris washed over them.

"Oh dear, my circuits simply can't take much more of this," C-3PO cried, as the ship shook beneath him. "At least the situation can't become any more dire."

Han slammed a fist against the control panel. "Don't you know better than to jinx us with —" A blaring alarm drowned out the rest of his words, and the air thickened with a foul gray smoke. "What was that?" C-3PO cried.

Han groaned. "*That* was the situation about to get more dire. A *lot* more."

Chewie's panicked bark came through the comlink.

"What'd he say?" Luke asked, feeling a little green around the edges as the ship swayed and bucked beneath him.

Han ignored him because he was busy keeping the ship from getting blown to bits. Without thinking, Luke clenched his hand around the hilt of his lightsaber. Not that this was the kind of danger he could take on with the laser sword, but reaching for it had become instinctual. The Jedi weapon usually made him feel stronger, ready to meet whatever challenge lay ahead.

Now it just made him feel useless. Luke could neither fly the ship nor repair it, and although Leia was pale with tension, she'd made it clear she didn't need his help either. He could do nothing but watch.

"Chewbacca says the shields are at ten percent power," C-3PO translated. "And that—*oh dear*. And that one more big hit and we're finished!"

"Then we'll just have to make sure we don't hit anything, won't we?" Han said through gritted teeth.

The *Millennium Falcon* rocketed up in a nearly ninety-degree climb, shooting past one pitted asteroid, then squeezing through the narrow gap between two more, with meters to spare.

"Watch out!" Leia cried.

"*Watching*," Han muttered. "Now strap in and keep quiet unless you want to fly this bird yourself!"

A string of chirps and beeps came through the comlink.

C-3PO tapped Han's shoulder. "Excuse me, captain, I hate to trouble you with additional bad news, but if you have a moment I feel I should relay—"

Han groaned. "Spit it out, you rusty circuit brain!"

"The deflector shields are down," C-3PO reported.

The ship shook with such force it felt like it was going to fly apart. And that's if they were *lucky*: At this speed, without deflectors, even a fist-sized rock could punch through a porthole and depressurize the ship. If it hit the engines, or the laser cannons . . .

Luke told himself he was overreacting. Surely if things were that bad, Han would let them know it was time to panic.

"Get your vac suits on!" Han shouted. "Initiate emergency procedures."

Time to panic. Luke jumped out of the co-pilot seat, then froze. "Han—"

"No time to chat, kid," Han snapped. "*Go.*"

"But Han—"

Han whipped the ship hard to port. "Even the Jedi can't breathe in a vacuum, kid. Trust me. Get your suit."

Luke grimaced. Did Han have to be so *stubborn*, even at a time like this? He was laser-focused on the tiny pocket of space just ahead. It may have been the only way to steer the *Falcon* on its narrow path to safety. But it meant he was missing the big picture. "Han," Luke said firmly. "*Look.*"

The path ahead of them was almost entirely clear. The debris field lay behind them. Delaya hovered in the distance, a globe of bluish-violet gleaming in the light of the sun.

Han's face stretched into a crooked grin. "See? Nothing to worry about."

But Luke's relief lasted only a moment. Leia was staring blankly through the side port at the receding debris. It had to be hard, seeing everything she'd lost. Luke searched himself for the right words, *something* that would help. But he had nothing.

An awkward silence settled over the cockpit.

Finally, Han cleared his throat. "Princess, we'll be landing in about fifteen minutes. Unless you want some time . . ."

She jerked her head away from the window and glared at him. "More time? I think we've wasted quite enough time on your flyboy stunts. Let's get to work."

Tobin Elad slipped into his cabin, shut the door behind him, and ceased to exist.

The man who bore his name — when it suited him — sat down in front of his comlink. But he paused before switching it on, taking a moment to soak in the silence of isolation.

It wouldn't be accurate to say he enjoyed the solitude.

The man didn't *enjoy* anything. Nothing made him *happy* or *sad* or *angry*. Emotions were for the weak, for the living. And despite the fact that his heart pumped blood and his lungs filtered air, the man was as dead and empty on the inside as a corpse.

The Commander had seen to that.

He opened a secure channel to the Imperial Center. Almost instantly, Commander Rezi Soresh's face appeared on the screen.

"X-7, report," he ordered.

The Commander had stripped away everything that had once been his life, every face, every name, every memory that had marked him as an individual being. The Commander had emptied him out, and given him only two things in return.

One, a name: X-7. A number, like a droid. Fitting for a creature that lived and breathed only to serve his master's orders. For that was the second thing he'd been given.

Desire. To serve the Commander's every whim. Nothing more.

Never anything less.

"The *Millennium Falcon* is ferrying Leia to Delaya, in the Alderaan system," X-7 reported in his true voice, blank and toneless. Tobin Elad, the man he was pretending to be, spoke in a dry voice that carried hints of his tragic past. The voice, like the words, had been carefully crafted to gain Leia's trust. But the voice, like the words, like the man, was an act. "The Delayan government has agreed to host her without notifying the Empire of her presence."

"A mistake," the Commander said, his hologram snapping into view, "but a useful one. And why has she come?"

"Delaya has become a gathering point for Alderaanians who were offworld at the time of the attack. Officially, Leia is here as their leader. She will offer help to the refugees and pay tribute to the memory of the dead."

"And unofficially?" the Commander prompted.

"She plans to recruit as many refugees as she can for the Rebel cause."

"Good," the Commander said. A ghost of a smile crossed his narrow, pinched face. "This we can use. And your mission?"

"I am closing in on a target. Leia trusts me. They all do. It's only a matter of time before they reveal the name of the pilot who destroyed the Death Star."

The Commander's smile grew wider. "And once we have confirmation?"

"The target will be eliminated," X-7 said. "If and when the Commander wills it."

"You are in a position to do so, when the time comes?" the Commander asked. "Without getting caught?"

Without intending to, X-7 allowed a hint of Tobin Elad's cocky certainty to creep into his voice. "With all due respect, sir, ferreting out the pilot's name will require some finesse. Killing him? That's the easy part."

elaya may have looked blue from a distance, but up close, it was nothing but gray. Leilani, its capital city, was packed with faceless duracrete factories puffing black smoke into the smog. Alderaan had long ago exported its manufacturing facilities to Delaya, and the centuries had taken their toll. Landspeeders clogged the narrow streets, creeping past rows of half-constructed buildings. Durasteel scaffolding flanked their exteriors, but the construction equipment sat abandoned.

"New factories," General Carlist Rieekan said, as he drove deeper into the city toward their lodgings. He had collected Leia from the spaceport; the others were following behind in a second landspeeder. Leia had wanted some time to talk to the general in private. "Or, they were supposed to be. There's no need for them now."

The Rebel General had been on a Delayan transmission station when Alderaan was destroyed, and had spent the last several weeks assisting refugee efforts around the sector. Tens of thousands of Alderaanians had been off planet when the Death Star struck. They had kept their lives — but lost everything else. "The Delayan economy has been troubled for years. But now? The planet generates most of its income from exporting goods to Alderaan. Without Alderaan . . ."

"No demand for goods," Leia finished for him.

"And no need for factories or workers to produce them," General Rieekan added, as they drove past a sidewalk crowded with humans and aliens. Leia spotted a Rodian, a Besalisk, three Bothans, and a cluster of white-tufted Ryn. They waited in a line that stretched around the block. "These stragglers came from all over the galaxy, looking for work. Now they have to rely on the government to feed and clothe them — or find another planet."

"Is it like this all over?" Leia asked. The General had spent much of the last couple weeks in other parts of Delaya, visiting refugees across the globe.

He nodded. "Alderaan's tragedy is borne by Delaya as well."

"All the more reason to be grateful to them for taking in the refugees," Leia said.

General Rieekan didn't respond.

"General?" she asked. He was a man who chose his words carefully, but when he did speak, it was always worth hearing.

"I don't want to influence you."

She smiled. "I can assure you, general, no one has ever accused me of being easily influenced."

The general sighed. "There are those here who feel their planet's resources should be reserved for Delayans. Prime Minister Manaa and his deputy, Var Lyonn, have sworn their willingness to help the refugees," he said.

"But?" she prompted him.

"It's just a bad feeling I have," he admitted. "Manaa's men follow me everywhere, and my interactions with the refugees are carefully supervised." He glanced out the window, nodding at a silver landspeeder off to their right. "Even now, they're following us. I've been told it's for security purposes."

"You suspect otherwise."

The general pulled up in front of a tall gray building and brought the landspeeder to a stop. The sign read *Delayan Whisperpines Hotel,* though there were no whisperpines — or any other tree — in sight. Leia would have preferred more modest accommodations, but the Delayan government had insisted on giving her the royal treatment. It seemed ungrateful to object. Especially since she was counting on them to keep this visit a secret from the Empire.

"I do," he said. "Perhaps I should have spent less time traveling. If I had looked deeper into the situation in Leilani . . ."

· "You've done all you can and more," she assured him. "And on behalf of the people of Alderaan, I thank you for your efforts."

"My efforts." He shook his head and pressed his fingers to his temples. "Your Highness, when the Death Star approached, I heard the distress cries from the transmission station — and I did nothing."

"There was nothing you could have done," Leia assured him. "There would have been no time to evacuate the planet, and if you had acted, you could have revealed Alderaan's connections to the Alliance. You had no way of knowing what the Empire was about to do."

Unlike me, she thought. *I knew exactly what was going to happen. I just couldn't stop it.*

"*You* are not to blame," she said firmly. "For any of this."

He inclined his head toward her slightly, acknowledging her words, if not agreeing with them.

As they climbed out of the landspeeder, a young man approached, running his hands nervously through his spiky black hair. The General smiled and waved him over. "Leia, meet Kiro Chen," he said. "He's been an invaluable help to the cause these last few weeks."

Leia looked warily at the stranger. "When you say 'the cause,' you mean . . ."

"He knows your true purpose here," General Rieekan explained. "He came to me as a representative of the survivors, hoping for a way to serve the Alliance."

Kiro gave Leia a firm handshake. "It doesn't make sense to talk about 'survivors' as a single group," he explained. "There are too many of us. Though it's only been a short time, different groups have formed — communities, really. Each with their own unofficial leaders."

"Like you?" Leia asked.

Kiro chuckled. "I'm no leader. I just pay attention. I know things. Like the fact that the Rebel Alliance is our greatest hope. If we want to stop another Alderaan . . ."

Leia winced. "It pains me that our planet's very name has come to stand for destruction and death," she said softly.

"Not all it stands for, your highness." Kiro smiled sadly. "You'll see to that."

"Not me," Leia said. "The Alliance."

The general nodded. " Exactly. Kiro is based here in Leilani, and he's managed to put together a coalition of survivors who might be willing to assist the Rebel efforts."

"They're hesitant," Kiro admitted. "After . . . what happened, they have good cause to be terrified of the Empire."

"All the more reason to fight," Leia said.

Kiro nodded. "I agree. And now that you're here, I know they'll commit. They . . . we —" he reddened — "have always drawn strength from your resolve."

As a princess and Imperial senator, Leia had grown quite skillful at accepting compliments. But this one touched her more deeply than most. "On behalf of the Rebel Alliance, I thank you for all you've done," she told him, aware she sounded overly formal. "I look forward to working together."

"I've been called for an operation in the Orus Sector," General Rieekan said. "And —"

"Can we have a moment, please?" Leia asked Kiro. He may have been one of her people, and General Rieekan may have trusted him, but he was still a stranger.

He backed away, leaving Leia and the general to speak privately.

"If you need me here, Your Highness, of course I'll stay."

Leia shook her head. "Go ahead. The Rebellion needs you more than I do."

"Just watch yourself," he warned her. "Minister Manaa may be the official head of the government, but his deputy, Var Lyonn, holds the true power. And the man is not to be trusted."

"Few are," Leia pointed out. "It's why the Rebel Alliance is lucky to have men like you."

"And like your father," he said quietly. "I grieve your loss."

Leia looked down. "It's a loss felt by all," she said brusquely. "And I intend to make sure we never suffer another one like it."

Leilani was corroded with rust, its air fouled with chemicals and its skies black with smoke. But when they arrived at the housing development that had been erected for Alderaan survivors, Leia was surprised to find everything shiny and new. There were even a few trees poking up between the small homes.

After introducing her to the Prime Minister and his deputy, General Rieekan had returned to the spaceport. At Leia's request, the government officials had brought her to see the accommodations that had been made for her people. Though she had wanted to go alone, Luke had insisted on coming along. He said he was curious, but she knew he just didn't want her to be alone. It infuriated her, the way everyone was treating her like she was some fragile piece of transparisteel, about to shatter into a million pieces. Yes, she'd lost everything — but she certainly wasn't the only one.

"There are two hundred residents in the T'iil Blossom Homes," Deputy Minister Var Lyonn said, proudly showing off the facilities. His gray shimmersilk robe, the same color as his thinning hair, brushed against the ground as he walked. "Families who were off planet on vacation, businessmen, students on school trips — every survivor has a different story, though of course they all end in the same tragic way. It's been our honor as Delayans to offer a safe and happy refuge."

Leia smiled at the groups of survivors picnicking in a ragged patch of grass. It reminded her of lazy afternoons on the grounds of the palace, snacking on Memily's custard bread while she watched the gingerbells bloom. The memory was as welcome as it was painful.

"We have established developments like this all across the city," Var Lyonn said. His smile didn't quite reach his eyes. Prime Minister Gresh Manaa, who hadn't spoken since he'd first introduced himself, nodded eagerly. He was shorter and rounder than his deputy, with a fringe of gray hair ringing his bulging chin. His wide eyes made him seem perpetually surprised. He walked a few feet behind Var Lyonn, like a child trailing his minder.

They rounded a hedge to discover a small boy huddled on the ground. When he spotted them, he wiped the tears from his eyes with two balled fists. "I'm not crying," he said defiantly.

"I can see that," Leia assured him. "Where are your parents?"

"In building seven," he said. "I got lost."

"Princess, we should really keep moving," Var Lyonn said. "We have much to see."

Leia ignored him. "Would you like help finding your parents?" she asked the child.

The boy burst into tears.

Var Lyonn grunted with impatience. "Your Highness, surely we all have more pressing matters to attend to than *baby-sitting*."

"Then you attend to them," Leia said, with as much politeness as she could muster. "*I'm* getting this child back to his family."

"As I've already explained, it's not safe for you to wander around on your own. If you insist, we can all —"

"You go," Luke said, catching her eye. "I remember passing building seven on our way in. It's just across the park."

"Excellent," Var Lyonn said brusquely, already walking away. "Rejoin us when you can." Leia nodded at Luke, and followed behind the Deputy Minister. It was clear he didn't want her out of his sight. At least this way, Luke would have a chance to do some exploring on his own.

"We've done what we can with the funds we have," Lyonn said, as they continued to stroll across the grounds, "but of course, the more we have, the more we can help." A number of wealthy former residents of Alderaan had donated funds to Delaya, to help them tend to the survivors. Although the Organa fortune had been pledged to the Rebellion, Leia knew of many who would donate funds at her request.

They wandered through narrow, tree-lined paths dotted with small buildings. There was a cultural center, a cafeteria, even a school. It looked like a comfortable place to live — but Leia suspected that for its residents, it would never be home.

"Time to go," Var Lyonn said, after they'd been there for less than an hour. "I don't know where your associate has wandered off to, but we'll collect him on our way out."

"Already?" She'd spoken to only a few of the survivors, all quick to thank the Delayan officials for giving them a new home. They seemed reluctant to say anything more. "You go. I can find my own way back."

"That would be ill advised," Lyonn said. "You're a very public figure — with a lot of enemies."

"I'm not concerned."

Lyonn and Manaa shared a look. "I'm afraid we don't have that luxury," Lyonn said, his tone civil but firm. "If something were to happen to you here, we would never forgive ourselves." He paused. "Of course you'll want us to take every precaution against having the Empire learn of your presence here."

It was only his cold smile that made it sound like a threat.

"I should probably return to the hotel anyway," Leia said gracefully. "I do need to prepare for tomorrow."

This was partly true. She had agreed to officiate at a large memorial ceremony. Hundreds of people would attend, all expecting her words to heal her wounds. She couldn't even heal her own.

But that wasn't why she agreed to return to the hotel. General Rieekan had been right: Manaa and Lyonn were hiding something. Picking a fight wouldn't be the best way to find out what it was. That was Han's way. Shoot first, ask questions never. Leia was more patient — but no less determined.

"You sure this is the right place?" Luke asked. Once they'd found building seven, the small boy had led him around to a playground in the back, claiming his parents would be waiting for him. But there was no one there. The boy looked more terrified than ever.

"Don't worry," Luke said. "We'll find your parents. They're probably out looking for you right at this moment."

"I didn't want to do it," the boy said.

"Do what?" Luke asked in confusion — and then rough hands grabbed him from behind, twisting his hands behind his back. A bag dropped over his head. Luke kicked out blindly, and his foot slammed hard into someone's stomach. There was a loud grunt, and his legs were kicked out from beneath him. He dropped to the ground, his head slamming into the duracrete.

"Careful, don't hurt him!" someone snapped.

Luke was scooped up and tossed onto a hard surface. There was a loud bang just over his head, like a lid being slammed shut. An engine rumbled, and the floor vibrated beneath him. It looked like he was going for a ride.

Like it or not.

Luke strained against the wrist binders. They wouldn't give. He twisted his arms toward his right hip, straining his fingers toward his belt. The men had taken his blaster — but they hadn't thought to search for other weapons. If he could just reach the hilt of his lightsaber . . .

There!

Luke was about to activate the blade, when he hesitated. It wasn't just the close quarters — he knew he might miss the binders and slice off a limb — it was a feeling, almost an inner voice, urging him to stop.

Have patience. Watch. Wait.

It was the kind of thing Ben might have said — but this wasn't Ben's voice. It came from somewhere deep inside of him. It was less a voice than a certainty that he should allow events to play themselves out.

Is it the Force? Luke wondered.

Or was it just his own fear?

Either way, Luke decided to listen. He still had his lightsaber. When the time came to use it, he would be ready. Until then, he would have patience. Watch.

Wait.

The lid swung open. Luke squinted into the light. Two figures stood over him, silhouetted by the sun, their faces hidden in shadow.

"We don't want to hurt you," the taller one said.

"And we won't — if you come quietly," added the other. "If you don't . . ." He left the threat unspoken.

"Where are we?" Luke asked.

Instead of answering, they yanked him out of the speeder, holding him upright as his legs buckled. Though his muscles quickly recovered, he let himself sag as they half-pushed, half-dragged him down the narrow path.

Let them believe he was weak.

"You're making a mistake," Luke warned, as they approached a massive building of faceless gray ferrocrete. Several similar structures stood on either side. Luke suspected they'd brought him to the warehouse district. But why? "If you tell me what you want, maybe we can work something out."

"We got what we wanted," the shorter man growled. "You."

Once again, Luke considered going for his lightsaber. Here, the odds were one against two. Not great, since the two had blasters and all he had was a lightsaber he could barely use.

Watch.

Wait.

It defied sense, but Luke trusted his instincts. Just as Ben had instructed him.

The men shoved him into the building. Off balance, he stumbled through the door, toppling forward. They caught him just before he hit the ground and jerked him upright. Luke gasped.

It was a warehouse, as he'd guessed. But the only thing stored in this warehouse were people.

People everywhere — hundreds of them, perhaps a thousand. Sprawled on thin mats, leaning against the walls, sickly and pale. Huddled under threadbare blankets, fighting over foil-wrapped protein supplements. The building was hundreds of meters wide and at least six stories high, with landings on each level circling a wide open central area. The thick air stunk of rotting bantha meat.

"What is this place?" Luke whispered, forcing himself not to turn away from all the gaunt, hopeless faces.

"New Alderaan," one of his captors said bitterly. "Home sweet home."

"You can sit."

Luke's captors had shoved him into a small makeshift enclosure, bounded by two hanging sheets and a few thin sheets of plasteel propped against each other. The man facing him had a round face dusted by a reddish gold beard. Laugh lines framed his wide mouth, but the eyes beneath the bushy blond eyebrows shone with sorrow. "I said, *sit.*"

When Luke didn't move, his captors each put a hand on one of his shoulders, and forced him to the ground. He sat awkwardly, his arms still pinned behind him.

The bearded man glanced at the others. "Leave us."

The short, stocky one frowned. "Nahj, it's not safe."

The seated man gave him a thin smile. "I hardly think he poses much of a threat. And —" He gave Luke a pointed look. "He knows you'll be standing just outside, blasters at the ready. He's no fool. Are you?"

Luke said nothing.

The men nodded, and slipped out of the lean-to.

"You can call me J'er Nahj," the bearded man said, once they were alone. "And you are?"

Luke didn't answer.

"You're wondering why they brought you here," Nahj said.

"They did it because you told them to," Luke guessed.

"Not exactly." He sighed. "Not you."

Luke's eyes widened. He should have realized. "You were trying to kidnap *Leia*?" A flush of anger rose in him, and he readied himself to go for his lightsaber.

J'er Nahj looked abashed. "I'm not a bad man, you know. I'm hardly in the business of kidnapping."

"Then what kind of business are you in?"

"Before?" J'er Nahj raised his eyebrows. "I sold durasteel fixtures for 'freshers. You wanted a new sink or a fancy shower? I was your man. Outfitted 'freshers all over the sector. Before. Now ask me, 'Before what?'"

"I don't have to," Luke said. He still didn't understand why he was here, but it was painfully obvious why the rest of them were. "*Before* Alderaan. You're all survivors, aren't you?"

J'er Nahj barked out a harsh laugh. "Survivors? Didn't you hear? There were no survivors. An entire planet, gone in an instant. There were those of us who were off-planet, yes. Those of us who were at a 'fresher convention on Delaya while our wives were vaporized in the middle of cooking a pot of L'lahsh, our children blown to bits while running through the meadow picking t'iil blossoms. There were those of us who escaped," he said fiercely. "But make no mistake. None of us *survived*."

'm sorry," Luke said. "But the Delayan government had offered to help you. You don't need —"

"Who do you think shoved us into this the thousand in the warehouse next to this one, and the warehouse next to *that*. The Delayan government cares nothing for us. Whatever lies they may tell your princess."

"She's *your* princess," Luke said quietly.

"Then why does she let us suffer like this, while she dines with the Delayan space-slugs who left us here?"

"Because she doesn't *know*," Luke insisted.

"She had her chance to find out," Nahj snapped. "I requested an audience as soon as I found out she was coming. Her response made her feelings perfectly clear: Meeting with people like us is beneath her."

"But we never even got your request!" Luke protested, his thoughts spinning. The Delayan officials must have intercepted Nahj's message. Of course: They were trying to keep Leia from finding out about this place. "You've been lied to — but so have we."

"Politicians believe what they want to believe," Nahj scoffed. "The Delayans have only opened their planet to us so they can get their hands on what's left of Alderaan's wealth. Your Princess Leia will only acknowledge the truth if we force her to see it."

"Except that you ended up with the wrong hostage," Luke pointed out. "So what are you supposed to do now?"

"True, we don't have the princess," Nahj admitted. "But perhaps we have something she wants."

"Me?"

"It's an honest trade. She comes to us, she looks suffering in the face without turning away — and she gets you back, unharmed. If she doesn't care about you enough to come . . ."

"You'd . . . what?" Luke asked, eyeing the plasteel separating him from the men with blasters. "Kill me?"

Nahj winced.

"I don't think so," Luke said. "The people of Alderaan love peace. They still love it. And I think, despite all this, you're a peaceful man."

"Alderaan *was* a peaceful planet," a woman's voice said from behind Luke. "Until the princess and her father dragged it into war. Now we bear the consequences of *her* rash actions. It seems only right she should bear some of her own."

"Halle, please," Nahj said in a stony voice.

Luke twisted around to see a woman with short crimson hair, her mouth an angry red slash across her face. She was only a couple years older than Luke. "I didn't come here to fight," she said, looking like she regretted that fact. "Shell's outside. He wanted me to bring him over, to apologize."

Nahj nodded his permission.

"Shell!" she called out. "He says okay. You can come in."

Nothing happened. "One second," Halle said, slipping through an opening in the sheet.

"You can do it," Luke heard a man say. "It'll only be hard until you get the first word out — then, easy as skinning a nerf."

"He doesn't have to if he doesn't want to," Halle snapped.

"I want to," a young boy's voice said. A familiar voice.

"Good boy," the man said.

"You'll make him soft," Halle complained.

"No softer than you, deep down," the man said. "Even if you won't admit it." There was a long silence. When Halle reappeared, her cheeks were glowing, and her fingers strayed across her lips. But the smile disappeared as soon as she caught Luke watching her. "This is Shell," she said, slinging an arm around a young boy with brown hair and a familiar frown. "I believe you two know each other."

Luke still couldn't believe they'd used a child as bait.

"Sorry I lied to you," the boy said. He looked much less helpless than he had at the T'iil Blossom Homes, but no less miserable. "They weren't gonna hurt you or anything. They said it was the right thing to do."

"Lying is never the right thing to do," Luke said.

Halle scowled. "The kid's sorry," she spat out. "The *least* you can do is forgive him."

"I do forgive him," Luke shot back. "He's a child. What's your excuse?"

"Shell, go outside," Halle said tightly. "I'll be there in a minute."

"Halle . . ." Nahj's voice held a warning. "Maybe you should go, too."

"Maybe you should get *on* with things," Halle said.

"You don't have to do this," Luke told them. "Let me go, and I'll bring her to you myself. As soon as Leia sees all this, she'll want to help."

"Let you go?" Halle grimaced. "So you can run back to your princess and have us all arrested?"

"Leia will want to help," Luke promised. "Do you really want to teach your son that blackmail and kidnapping is the right way to fix things?"

"My *son*?"

"Shell is no one's son," Nahj said quietly. "His family was murdered on Alderaan. He was here visiting his grandmother, but the shock of the attack was too much for her and . . . He's on his own now. We all look after him. Him and the others."

An orphan.

Luke saw the smoking remains of the moisture farm on Tatooine, Aunt Beru and Uncle Owen's skeletons smoldering in the ruins.

Creating orphans was the Empire's specialty.

"I will help, if you let me," Luke said. "But this is not the way."

Nahj tightened his lips and looked away. Halle shook her head in disgust and rubbed a hand across her eyes.

Their gaze was only off him for a moment, but it was enough. Time seemed to draw itself out, slowing to a crawl. Luke twisted his arms around, grasping the hilt of his lightsaber. He activated the blade and, in one smooth, swift chop, sliced through the cords binding his wrists. He leapt to his feet, blade outstretched, its tip centimeters away from J'er Nahj's throat.

"Don't," Nahj said quietly. Luke realized he was speaking to Halle, who was about to lunge at him, despite the fact that she was unarmed.

"One scream," Halle warned Luke in a low voice, "and you're facing ten men with blasters."

"One centimeter," Luke said, glancing toward the lightsaber blade. "Are your men with blasters faster than my blade?" He had no intention of hurting Nahj, or any of them. But Halle had to believe he would.

Nahj shook his head. "We agreed no violence," he said, remarkably calm. He turned to Luke. "So what now?"

"Now?" Luke hesitated — then deactivated the lightsaber. Nahj emitted a barely noticeable sigh as the blue beam disappeared. "Now I contact Leia, and we try to find a way to help your people. Just as I said I would." He held out his hand. "One of your men took my comlink."

"Merely a precaution." Nahj pulled out his own comlink out from beneath his cloak and handed it to Luke. "Use mine."

"J'er!" Halle snapped. "If he calls in the authorities . . ."

Nahj ignored her. "Please," he told Luke. "If our methods were misguided, you must believe our motives were pure. We knew the princess would only be on Delaya for a short time, and that the government would do anything they could to prevent her from learning about our fate. We were desperate. We *are* desperate."

Luke flicked on the comlink.

"Luke!" Leia sounded relieved. "We've been looking everywhere for you! What happened? Is everything all right?"

Luke paused, meeting Nahj's searching gaze. Leia would be outraged if she learned the truth. She would never trust J'er Nahj — and that might get in the way of helping his people.

On the other hand, it felt wrong to lie to her.

What do I do? he asked silently, hoping that the mysterious certainty he'd felt earlier would return. But the Force, if that's what it had been, was silent. He was on his own.

"Everything's fine," he said steadily. "I just . . . decided to do a little exploring."

J'er Nahj breathed out the same quiet sigh he had when Luke pulled the lightsaber from his throat. Halle's scowl didn't fade.

"Are you on your way back?" Leia asked, still sounding anxious.

"Actually, I think you should join me here," Luke told her. "There's something you need to see."

You sure he didn't happen to mention what he was *doing* all the way out here?" Han asked, slogging through the muddy streets. If it *was* mud. It smelled more like raw sewage.

Leia shook her head. "Just said it was important that we come."

Han didn't have anything against the idea of coming to the rescue. Obviously the kid had gotten himself into some kind of trouble, as usual. Han just wished he'd found trouble a little closer to home.

Back at the hotel, they had autovalets, a greenputt course, fresh-squeezed juma juice, and bloody nerf steak — all paid in full by the Delayan government. Whereas here, on the outer edge of the city, all they had were abandoned construction sites, mounds of festering garbage, and sewage. Scrawny rodents with patches of greenish-yellow fur scampered in the gutters, and bludflies swarmed overhead. Han was sure he'd caught a glimpse of a borrat burrowing under a nearby building, at least two meters from tusk to tail. Not that Han had anything against life on the shady side of town — but a little luxury every once in a while never hurt.

The pubtrans flitter didn't even extend to this neighborhood, and the driver they'd hired had refused to drive them more than halfway. "You won't find anyone willing to take you to that part of town," he'd warned them. "You'd have to be crazy."

More like stubborn, Han thought, glancing at the princess. She'd just shrugged and insisted they walk. He didn't even know why he was still *on* this planet. *One more day,* he told himself. *Then I'm out.*

Chewbacca issued a low, gutteral growl. The Wookiee was crankier than usual.

"You *know* why you couldn't be the one to stay behind," Han said. "If that Deputy Minister or his cronies try to track down the princess, *someone* needs to be there and talk 'em out of it. And something tells me Elad will do the job better than two droids and a Wookiee."

They hadn't been forbidden from leaving the hotel — not exactly. But that was because they hadn't asked. They'd snuck out the window, leaving Elad and the droids behind to explain things if it was discovered they were gone.

Chewbacca growled again.

"Because I don't want them here, bugging me!" Han said. "The little one's okay, but that protocol droid . . ." He shook his head. "Let's just say the less time I spend with him, the less chance he has of getting turned into a scrap-pile."

The Wookiee let out a mournful groan.

"Not so bad?" Han exclaimed. "Easy for you to say. The rustbucket's terrified of you. Has some crazy idea you're going to rip off his arms."

Chewbacca barked out a reply.

"Well, okay, so I *am* the one who gave him that idea. I just wanted him to shut his mouth for five seconds. Can you blame me?" Han swore under his breath as his boot squished into something soft and pungent. It looked like it had once been alive — but he didn't look too close.

"Han," Leia said quietly.

"I know, I know." Han scowled down at his boot, trying to scrape off the worst of it. "The bag of bolts comes in handy sometimes. *Sometimes.*"

"No, Han. Look!"

Three men — *No,* he realized, *not men. Boys* — stood before them, blocking the narrow road. They stood mutely with their hands raised, palms up.

"What do you think they want?" Leia murmured. "Money?"

Han shot her a sharp look. Every once in a while, she said something that reminded him of the distance between them. It wasn't the kind you could cross in a ship. "Well, I doubt they're begging for the fun of it, Your Highness."

Without hesitating, Leia pulled out a pouch of credits, hurrying toward the boys. Something familiar about the setup clicked in Han's brain. "Leia, wait—"

Too late.

As she dropped a handful of credits into the tallest boy's outstretched hands, he snatched her wrist and twisted it behind her back. A rusted vibroblade appeared in his other hand. He held it to her throat.

"You kids crazy?" Han shouted. "You really want to face off against a *Wookiee*?"

To help get the point across, Chewbacca shook his furry fists in the air, roaring.

The other two kids looked nervous, but the one in charge didn't flinch. "Just give us all your credits and we'll leave you alone."

"And what makes you so sure we'll leave *you* alone?" Han shot back, his fingers twitching toward his blaster. Not that he'd shoot at a bunch of kids. But if he could scare them, or cause some kind of distraction . . .

He shook his head, tempted to laugh. Served him right, falling for such a worn-out stunt. He'd pulled it on more than a few clueless oldies himself back when he was a kid.

Not that he'd ever been dumb enough to attack a *Wookiee*.

"Do you know who I *am*?" Leia asked in an icy voice. "I'm —"

"Not the kind of gal who scares easy," Han said quickly. Talk about not having a clue. Did she really think it would *help* to tell them she was a princess? A *rich* princess? "And neither is my friend here."

Chewbacca roared again, louder this time.

"So how 'bout you put down the knife —"

"How bout *you* stop wasting my time, old man," the kid snarled, "and hand over the credits."

"*Old man*?" Han took a step forward. He didn't need a blaster. Not to handle this punk. Chewbacca growled. "No thanks, buddy," Han said. "This one's *all mine*."

Han didn't hear the footsteps behind him, and he didn't hear the blaster fire. He just saw the laser bolt slam into the kid's blade, centimeters from Leia's neck. It was a clean hit — the blade went flying. The kid backed away, examining his hand like he couldn't believe it was still in one piece.

Han couldn't believe it either. It was one of the cleanest shots he'd ever seen. He whirled around. A plump old man stood behind him, his jaunty grin mostly covered by a thick, graying beard. Han scoured the streets, convinced *this* couldn't be the guy who'd fired the shot. But there was no one else around.

And the old guy was holding a smoking blaster. "Thought we agreed you kids weren't going to do this anymore!" he called out.

The lead kid reddened and retrieved his blade, shoving it into his back pocket. "Wasn't planning to," the kid said sullenly. "Not my fault they showed up in this neighborhood. They were asking for it."

"Come on, Mazi," the man said sternly. "Try it again and the deal's off."

"Yeah. Fine." He glared at Han. "But I could've taken you, old man. No question." He nodded to his friends and, without a word, they slipped away into the darkness."

Han grinned. The kid had spunk, you had to give him that. "Friends of yours?" he asked the old man.

"I pay them to run errands for me, do odd jobs, and the like, as long as they promise to stay out of trouble. That's the deal." He was talking to Han — but all the while, he was staring at Leia.

She glared back. "You're alive," she said flatly.

The man looked down at himself, as if examining the evidence. "So it would seem."

Leia had never expected to see him again.

"Princess." He took a step toward her, his arms outstretched, then hesitated and dropped them to his sides. "I'd heard you were here."

"And I—" Leia stopped, overwhelmed by a swirl of conflicting emotions. "I thought you were still on Alderaan."

He smiled gently. "I had some business on Delaya. I arrived here the day before the attack."

"I'm glad," she said flatly.

"This guy a friend of yours, Highness?" Han said.

"No." The word came automatically.

"Fess Ilee," he said, shaking hands with Han and nodding toward Chewbacca. "I am a friend of Bail Organa's."

"He *was* a friend to my father," Leia clarified. "But my father is dead."

"I am and always will be his friend," Fess said steadily.

He was a man of soft, rounded edges, with a belly bulging over his belt and the makings of a double chin. His fingers were stubby, his nose bulbous, and his mind seemed to be as fuzzy as the back of his neck. Leia had never been sure of his age — most of the time, he looked far older than her father, weathered and weak. But there had been moments when, out of the corner of her eye, she caught him moving with a surprising grace, the years falling away from his suddenly youthful face.

He lacked every quality her father had possessed: nobility, courage, wisdom. Though he called himself a botanist, his main skill seemed to be currying favor.

He grinned and nodded with greasy ease, laughing heartily at the weakest joke, complimenting the gaudiest gown. And yet Bail Organa had spoken of him privately with respect.

"How are you?" Fess asked.

"How do you think?" Leia snapped. Then she steadied herself. As a princess and a Senator she'd grown adept at dealing gracefully with her enemies. And Fess wasn't an enemy, he was just a harmless parasite. "I'm fine," she said, more politely. "Thank you for helping us with those boys."

Fess shook his head. "I can't stand to see children forced to make a life for themselves on the streets."

He didn't sound like the Fess she remembered — but then, they were all different now.

"We should be going," Leia said.

"I'll come along," Fess suggested. "It's dangerous out here alone."

"I'm hardly alone," she said, glancing at Chewbacca, who towered over the humans by several feet. The Wookiee rumbled in agreement.

"I know this city," Fess argued. "I can be of assistance. Perhaps more than you know."

Han snorted. "What is it with you old men and your delusions of grandeur?" he muttered.

"Excuse me?"

"You just reminded me of someone else who thought we could use his help," Han said. "Didn't end so well for him."

"Perhaps he lacked my skill set," Fess said mildly. "But—as you wish."

As they said their goodbyes, Leia wondered if she would ever see him again, and if she cared.

She needn't have bothered. They were only a few blocks away when Han snuck a glance over his shoulder. "That's one stubborn old man."

Leia stopped short. "He's following us?" She whirled around, but the streets were empty.

"Ducks into an alley every time I look back," Han said. "Sneaky fellow, but not sneaky enough. Guess he doesn't know who he's dealing with, does he, Chewie?"

The Wookiee barked a yes.

"You want me to run him off?" Han asked.

Leia shook her head, and began walking again. "If he wants to follow us so badly, let him."

From everything she knew about Fess, she suspected his offers of assistance were as empty as his head. Still, there was a strange reassurance in knowing he was following her. As if some childish, irrational part of her believed what her father had once told her: that no harm would come to her as long as Fess Ilee was alive.

Fessssss," she hisses, laughing at the sound of it, wet and slimy like a Kowakian monkey-lizard. And that is what he looks like, she decides, with his greasy smile and those tufts of hair growing out of his big ears. "Fess the monkey-lizard."

"Shhh!" Winter urges her. "They'll hear us."

"Relax," Leia tells her best friend. "No one will find us here." They have hidden themselves at the edge of the grand ballroom, tucked behind a swooping marble staircase. Leia is supposed to be in the center of the room, swinging across the dance floor in a long ballgown of shimmersilk.

But that was before she and Winter hid a giant wooly moth in the Minister of Agriculture's desk drawer. He deserved it — but Leia's father didn't see it that way. (Especially after the wooly moth chewed through a sheet of flimsiplast containing the budget for the whole next year.) Now she is banned from attending the party —

but Leia has decided that doesn't mean she can't watch.

It's more fun here, anyway. They have a pile of scavenged food, from t'iil seed cake to spiced grazer loaf. And from where they sit, they can easily hear all the silly people trying to impress her father. Leia is only eight years old, but she knows that grinning and nodding and agreeing with everything he says isn't the way to do it.

They nibble on sticks of sweetened Oro bark and watch Groos Corado try to persuade Tasha Moore to dance. They giggle as brothers Cassio and Pol Prentiss argue about which of them cheats at greenputt. But worst of all is Fess Ilee. Leia has never heard anyone talk so much and say so little. No matter how many words spill out of his mouth, they all have the same meaning: Yes, you're right.

She glares at him — then gasps, as he swivels his head toward her hiding place. His gaze travels over the heads of the crowd and locks onto her. She knows she is totally hidden — but she can't shake off the feeling that he knows she is there.

"I'm bored," she whispers to Winter. "Let's get out of here."

But when she slips out of her hiding place, she walks right into her father. And he is not happy.

He doesn't yell. He simply banishes her to her room. Tomorrow, she is supposed to go with Winter to the gingerbell blossom festival, but now, according to her father, that is not going to happen.

That's what he thinks.

Leia waits until the house falls asleep. Then she opens her bedroom window and climbs onto the sill. Balancing carefully on the frame, she examines her options. There is a low hanging tree branch, its tip just out of reach. Even if she stretches as far as she can, it won't be enough. But if she jumps, she will be able to grab it. Unless she misses.

She never misses.

Leia launches herself at the branch, digging her fingers into the scratchy bark. She dangles for a moment, swinging her feet through the air, proud of her daring. Then, hand over hand, she pulls herself to the trunk and shimmies down to the ground.

She runs across the dark and empty palace grounds, laughing into the night air. She is free.

The city is different in the dark. The streets are abandoned. She doesn't know where she is going, but she doesn't care.

She doesn't hear the footsteps, doesn't notice the shadow following her through the night.

She is not afraid.

"You sure this is the place?" Han asked, as they arrived at the coordinates Luke had given them. "It's a dump." It was a massive duracrete warehouse, surrounded on all sides by mounds of trash. Much of Leilani seemed broken down and abandoned—but this looked condemned.

Leia glanced over her shoulder, but Fess had disappeared. She double-checked the coordinates. "This is it."

They stepped inside.

And into a nightmare.

How did this happen? Leia thought in horror, forcing herself to look into the desperate, hopeless faces of her people. *How could I let this happen?*

Since the destruction of Alderaan, she'd distracted herself with one Rebel mission after another, trying to bury her pain. Trying to forget.

But she'd never intended to forget the people who had been left behind.

"You were right, Manaa and Var Lyonn were hiding something," Luke said, appearing beside her. "This."

The man next to him, young, though his hair was streaked with gray, extended a hand. "J'er Nahj," he introduced himself. "The Delayan government didn't want you to see the reality of our situation, but Luke here thought you'd want to know."

"I ran into Nahj outside of the hotel," Luke said, giving the man an odd look. "He agreed to bring me here so I could see for myself."

"More than seven thousand of us, Your Highness," Nahj said. "That we know of. The lucky ones had credits stored off-planet, or family and friends they could rely on. The less fortunate were taken in by the government, given houses and resources and put on display, to impress people like you. To make sure the money keeps rolling in. But here you see what happens to those with no luck at all. The ones who find themselves alone in the galaxy, everyone they ever knew and everything they ever had destroyed. The ones who can no longer afford to feed themselves — or the ones who can no longer muster the will to do it, because they would rather be dead. We're a drain on the Delayan economy. And worse, we're a reminder of unhappiness. It's easier to dump us here and forget about us. Makes it easier for everyone to move on."

Leia clutched his hand. "I promise you this: No one is moving on. Not without you."

Luke swung the landspeeder abruptly to the left, veering around a corner, straight through a lane clogged with traffic. A luxury speeder behind them slammed on its brakes just in time.

"Luke, what are you doing?" Leia asked in alarm.

"I told you not to let the kid drive," Han grumbled.

J'er Nahj had offered them use of a landspeeder to return to the hotel. Luke didn't understand. "If you can afford a landspeeder, then can't you afford —" He broke off, looking around at the conditions in the warehouse, his question obvious.

"I'm not here out of need," Nahj had said. "I'm here because these are my people."

Luke knew he'd just come within meters of crushing Nahj's landspeeder (and its passengers), but it had been worth it. He'd confirmed his suspicions. "We're being followed," he said, glancing over his shoulder at the red SoroSuub X-31. It was keeping its distance, but it had matched every one of Luke's twists and turns.

Luke glanced at Leia, who still seemed a bit shaken up from what she'd seen at the warehouse. "We can contact Var Lyonn and have him waiting at the hotel with reinforcements," he suggested.

"That probably *is* Lyonn," Han argued. "Or one of his men."

"Maybe. Maybe not." With a dangerous smile, Leia narrowed her eyes at the SoroSuub speeder. "Let's find out."

Luke pushed the landspeeder as fast as it would go, whooshing through the streets of the warehouse district. He took a hairpin curve at full speed, nearly flipping the vehicle on its side. The speeder shot down a back alley, then burst out the other side, nearly slamming into a giant borrat frozen in the middle of the road, its furry ears twitching as it stared into the oncoming traffic. Veering around it, Luke skidded across the sidewalk and plowed through a detour sign blocking off the entrance to a street crowded with construction equipment. He threaded the landspeeder through a scrum of bulldozers and deactivated construction droids, his teeth rattling as the repulsorlifts bounced over the torn up road.

Still, the red SoroSuub followed. Leia's plan called for them to *look* like they were trying to evade their pursuer, even as they drew him deeper and deeper into the abandoned district. As far as Luke was concerned, her rash "plan" was more like a death wish. It sounded like something *Han* would have come up with. So Luke wasn't just pretending to evade pursuit. He was determined to shake the guy.

Just one problem: Whoever was following them seemed to anticipate Luke's every move.

"Turn in here!" Leia barked, and Luke swung the landspeeder sharply to the right, ducking into a narrow, twisting alley. It dead-ended in a high, durasteel gate with sharp barbs running along the top. "Perfect," Leia said. "Stop."

Luke groaned. *What was so perfect about a dead end?* But he obeyed her command and hit the brakes.

"Remind me of this brilliant plan again, Your Worshipfulness," Han said. "We're going to get out of the landspeeder, wait for this guy, whoever he is, to catch up with us, and — what, exactly?"

"And find out who he is and what he wants," Leia said. "You have a problem with that?"

"Let's see," Han said. "It's risky, it's foolish, it's overconfident—"

Chewbacca growled, and Han grinned at him. "Because you didn't let me *finish*, you overgrown fuzz-ball. I was about to say, sounds like my kind of plan."

"That's what I'm afraid of," Luke muttered.

The red SoroSuub pulled into the alley and drew to a stop.

"Got your blaster ready, kid?" Han asked.

Luke nodded. *But I'll only use it if I have to*, he thought, his hand straying to his lightsaber. According to Ben it was more effective than a blaster.

Of course, Ben had known how to use it.

A single figure slipped out of the red speeder, shrouded by the milky twilight. Han jumped out of the speeder, his blaster raised. Chewie followed, his bowcaster at the ready. Luke stayed in the speeder, determined to protect Leia at all costs. The man advanced with his arms out, no weapon drawn. Luke tensed. The man could be offering himself up in peace . . . or it could be a trap.

Leia groaned and reached for the door. Luke grabbed her wrist. "You promised you'd stay in the speeder until we figured out what was going on."

She shrugged him off. "I *know* what's going on." She pushed past him and climbed out of the speeder. Luke activated his lightsaber and rushed after her. "What are you doing, Fess?" she shouted. "You could have gotten us all killed."

"I need to talk to you," Fess said, approaching. "This seemed the best way."

Luke stepped in front of Leia and activated his lightsaber. "Next time, try a comlink."

The man froze, all color draining from his face.

"It's fine, Luke," Leia said from behind him. "It's just Fess. He's harmless."

"Interesting weapon you have there," Fess said, in a choked voice. "*Luke*, did you say?"

Luke glanced at Leia, ready to take her lead. She sighed, and her shoulders slumped.

"He's a friend, Luke," Han said. Leia glared at him. "Well, not a friend, exactly," Han added hastily. "But he's no danger to us."

"You want to talk, Fess?" Leia snarled. "Talk."

But Fess wasn't looking at her. His eyes were locked on Luke. He extended a hand and — not knowing what else to do, Luke shook it. A strange current passed between them. Luke jerked his hand away.

He reminds me of Ben, Luke thought. But that didn't make any sense. The two men had nothing in common. Obi-Wan Kenobi had been tall and gaunt, dressed in a ragged cloak, his frown hidden by a dense beard, his eyes piercing, Fess was nearly twenty years younger, his soft features rounded by a life of ease and plentiful food, clothed in fine robes, his face frozen in a false smile.

There had been no falseness in Ben. And yet . . .

What is it? Luke thought, frustrated. He didn't know if he was asking himself — or Ben. What is it about this man. This . . .

"Ferus?" The word popped out of his mouth before he realized what he was saying, as if someone else had spoken it.

Fess took an abrupt step backward, growing even paler.

"Ferus," Luke said again, filled with an inexplicable certainty. The word drifted through his mind like a whisper. He didn't know what it meant, but he somehow knew he was speaking truth.

"*No*," Fess said, with quiet intensity. "Not anymore."

Ferus Olin.

Not his name. Not anymore, not for a long time.

He'd left it behind, the day he arrived in Alderaan's seemingly infinite sea of grass. Created a new life for himself. Not that it was much of a life, tending to the nerfs, wandering the grasslands, trying not to think about everything he'd lost. Trying not to imagine the accusing faces of the dead.

Ry-Gaul.

Solace.

Garen Muln.

And Roan. It was Roan Lands's face that he saw when he woke, Roan's voice he heard when he drifted off to sleep.

Not that he slept much.

He was hiding, he knew that. He'd tried fighting the Empire, tried fighting Darth Vader — and one bad decision after another had led here. To a life of isolation, a life that wasn't a life, but a mission.

Protect Leia.

Living like a hermit may have worked for Obi-Wan, stranded on a dusty desert planet in the middle of nowhere. But Alderaan was a world of life and crowds, swirling with social networks. A world of meaningful connections. Which might have appealed to him once, back when he was Ferus Olin — former Jedi, former Bellassan security expert, former resistance fighter, former enemy of the Empire.

Now he was just *former*. He had made himself invisible, and invisible men can form no connection.

Invisible men can, however, blend in. Gradually, Ferus gave up his life in the grasslands for a new life in the city. Took on a new identity. *Fess*, a repugnant name for a repugnant man. It was the only way to stay close to Leia. Disappearing in plain sight meant becoming what he hated most. A man who said nothing that mattered. A man who held no opinions except the opinions of whoever he was speaking to. A man who lived his life on the surface, so empty of purpose and thought, so inconsequential that no one could suspect he had anything to hide.

He became a mirror, reflecting back what people wanted to see and hear, keeping his true self hidden so deeply he'd almost forgotten where to find it. And now

Luke Skywalker, of all people, had found it for him. Had somehow found *him.*

The Force was strong in Luke, but wild, like an untamed animal. And yet he had the lightsaber — Anakin Skywalker's lightsaber. Did he know the truth of its origin? Did he know about his father?

Did his father know about him?

No, Ferus thought. *He'd already be dead.*

Or worse.

Luke, Leia, and Han took him back to their quarters, treating him like a sick, weak old man. *And maybe they're right,* he thought, disgusted with himself. His Jedi training had made him adept at finding the calm center of any crisis. Yet here he was, allowing his emotions to overtake him, like an inexperienced Padawan.

Still, if his weakness gained him more time with Leia — with *Luke* — perhaps it was worth it. And so he smiled and nodded and allowed them to believe he needed their help.

"Luke Skywalker," he said, settling into a soft chair. "Unusual name." Luke and Leia hovered anxiously over him, while Han took a seat on the sofa. Across the room, another man leaned against the wall, casually scanning a datapad. At least, that's how the man wanted it to seem. But his dark eyes were fixed on Ferus, measuring his every move. "You're not from these parts, I suspect?"

Luke shook his head, his familiar smile a faint, terri-fying echo of the past.

Anakin had smiled rarely when Ferus was around, but occasionally even Ferus had caught glimpses of the boy's easy charm. It had been an excellent mask.

When they were boys together, Anakin had not yet taken his first steps down the path to the dark side. But there had always been something, hadn't there? Something only Ferus had sensed — something that called to the darkness.

Leia is his child, too, Ferus reminded himself. But it wasn't the same. There was no darkness inside of Leia, only light.

"Nowhere near these parts," Luke said, peering at Ferus like he was trying to solve a puzzle. "I'm from Tatooine."

That much, I knew, Ferus thought. *But how did you come to be* here? *And why didn't Obi-Wan warn me?*

That was Obi-Wan for you. The Jedi only dispersed information on a need-to-know basis. And he seemed to feel there was little Ferus needed to know.

He hadn't heard from Obi-Wan in more than a year. Ferus had contacted him after the destruction of Alderaan, but Obi-Wan had responded to none of his transmissions. "You're very far from home," Ferus said. "You must miss it."

Several emotions flashed across Luke's face. Grief. Regret. Guilt.

Luke chose determination. "I'm where I need to be. It's like Ben said—" He stopped abruptly, shaking his head.

"Ben?" Ferus prompted him, something clenching in his chest. Years before, he had visited Obi-Wan on Tatooine. The Jedi Master lived as a hermit in the desert wasteland, but he had occasionally traded with some of the local creatures. They had called him by a different name. *Ben.*

Luke glanced at Leia, as if reminding himself that Ferus was not to be trusted. Ferus felt something in the boy shut down. "It's nothing," he said quickly. "Just something an old friend of mine used to say."

"Is he with you on Delaya? Can I meet him?" Ferus realized he was sounding too eager. "To thank him for protecting her highness," he added with more restraint. "As I thank all of you."

Luke looked down. "He's dead."

A shock wave crashed over Ferus, drowning out all sound, sight, and thought. The thought was unbelievable, *unacceptable.*

This "Ben" could have been anyone, he thought. There was no evidence linking him to Obi-Wan. Ferus wanted to grab for the tiny sliver of hope—but the Jedi in him rebelled against denying the truth.

And the truth was, some part of him had already known. Hadn't *wanted* to know, but known nonetheless.

Obi-Wan was gone. Ferus was alone.

He realized there was a glass of water in his hand. Lost in his daze, he hadn't even noticed the watchful stranger cross the room. Now the man knelt before him, peering intently into his eyes. "You went rather pale again — perhaps it would help to drink something."

Ferus shrank away from the man's touch. There was something in him — not *wrong*, but missing.

"And you are?" Ferus asked, his voice creaking like he hadn't used it in years.

"Tobin Elad," the man said, offering a hand to shake. Ferus forced himself to accept.

The Force flowed through every being in the galaxy. Good or evil, they all pulsed with different shades of the same energy. But there were a few beings in the galaxy who, for reasons even the Jedi didn't understand, lived beyond the energy flow. They couldn't be categorized into light or dark — they were simply null points, empty, as if they didn't exist.

This man existed, but the Force flowed *around* him, not through him. Nothing could penetrate the hollow at his center.

Ferus released the man's hand with poorly disguised relief. Touching him had been like grasping a puff of cold air.

"You're ill," Leia said, torn between annoyance and concern. "Is there someone we can call for you?"

Not anymore, he thought sourly, shaking his head.

But that wasn't true, was it? He wasn't alone in the galaxy, not with Luke and Leia standing before him. He need only speak the truth of their united past, reveal himself as a Jedi . . . It would be a shock for Leia, but perhaps it was time. Wasn't it wrong of him to deny her the truth, that most powerful weapon?

No.

The voice came from inside his head and outside at the same time.

Have patience.

Obi-Wan's voice.

Was his grief so deep that he'd conjured an imaginary Obi-Wan, complete with Obi-Wan's maddening caution? Was it a manifestation of the Force?

Or was it Obi-Wan himself, dead and yet somehow still alive?

The time will come to speak the truth, the voice said. *But not yet. Trust me.*

For whatever reason, Ferus did.

Why doesn't he tell them? X-7 thought. He could tell from the look in Fess's eye, the tension in his spine, the careful way he avoided touching X-7 when they brushed past each other — Fess knew something was up.

But he said nothing.

Interesting, X-7 thought. *But how did he know?*

This was the troublesome part. X-7's disguise was perfect. Certainly it should have taken more than a glance and a handshake for the stranger to see through him. As time passed, the struggle to maintain his disguise was proving to be more and more exhausting. Had he finally slipped?

Perhaps it was simpler than that: After all, one fraud can almost always recognize another.

And if X-7 was sure of anything, it was this: Fess Ilee was a fraud.

Fooling most people was easy—you just manipulated their emotions, showed them what they wanted to see. But X-7 had no emotions, and X-7 wanted nothing. Not in the normal sense, at least.

Which meant he couldn't be fooled in the normal sense.

Apparently this Fess, whoever he was—whatever he was—couldn't be fooled, either.

If you're smart, you'll stay out of my way, X-7 thought. *If not, I'll find out who you really are.*

And then I'll know how to destroy you.

CHAPTER TEN

He watches her climb out the window and leap nimbly to the ground. She sprints into the shadows.

He follows.

Ferus knows he could alert Bail Organa to his daughter's departure — but that is not his job. He is only to observe and, when necessary, protect.

He has observed a smart, headstrong girl. Too stubborn and too careless, with a fierce sense of justice. He has seen her pick a fight with a boy twice her size, avenging the ill treatment of a wounded thranta. He has watched her do battle with her father over etiquette and homework and when she will be permitted to accompany him to Coruscant — but none of the arguments have changed the fact that she adores him, studies every move Bail Organa makes, wants to be just like him when she grows up.

It is Ferus's job to make sure she has the chance.

Just a job, *he reminds himself constantly. Leia charms everyone around her. Such a serious face, such an intense will, in such a young girl. But Ferus knows well the dangers of growing attached. It blinds the senses, dulls the instincts. Leia has a large family, a full staff, an entire* planet *of people to love her. But she has only one who is solely dedicated to protecting her. Love is just a distraction.*

The shadows appear just as she approaches the deserted marketplace. For a second, Ferus imagines he sees a pack of wild taopari stalking the young princess. Then his vision resolves itself: They are men, three of them.

But they are stalking her nonetheless.

She notices nothing. She is nearly skipping down the street, arms outstretched to the darkness. He can feel the joy rolling off her in waves. Her anger at her father has dissipated, leaving behind a pure exuberance at being alone in the night. She is free, and the freedom is forbidden, making it all the sweeter.

She doesn't sense the danger — but Ferus can. He activates his lightsaber. The blue blade shimmers in the night. Ferus stretches out with the Force, and the men's whispers tickle his ears as if he is standing invisibly in their midst.

"Too risky, it's got to be a trap."

"Don't be paranoid, she's on her own. Now's our chance."

"She's just a kid; they wouldn't let her out alone like this."

"Exactly, she's a kid, she probably ran away. They might not even know she's gone yet, and by the time they do, we'll be long gone."

"It's still a risk."

"No risk, no reward. And Senator Aak's going to pay big."

"Bold move, using Organa's daughter to blackmail him."

"Bold and brilliant — if the Senator gets the kid, Organa will vote however he wants. His power's gone."

"We're not gonna hurt her, right? She's a kid."

"You said that already."

"No, we're not gonna hurt her."

"As long as she behaves."

Ferus strikes. He streaks through the dark night, invisible but for his glowing blade. The blade swoops down in a graceful arc, slicing through the largest man's blaster. In a single, fluid move, Ferus whirls around and jabs his foot into a soft, fleshy stomach. There is a quiet "oooof," and the second man drops to the ground. Ferus steps down hard on his wrist, forcing him to drop the laser pistol he's just retrieved.

The third man strikes at Ferus's head. The blaster hilt slams into his skull. Before Ferus can protect himself, another blow lands. There is sharp crack of durasteel on bone. *Ferus stumbles backward, dazed. His vision clouds over.*

That shouldn't have happened, *he thinks, lashing out blindly with his lightsaber. Perhaps the years of inaction have left him soft. Clumsy. Perhaps his connection with the Force is weakening. It wouldn't be the first time.*

A laser bolt whizzes by, close enough that he can feel the heat against his cheek. He raises his lightsaber, stretching instinctively toward the incoming blasts. As he breathes in deeply, trying to absorb the throbbing pain in his head, blast after blast sparks off the glowing blade.

One of the men he's knocked to the ground is climbing to his feet. He lunges toward Ferus.

"No!" shouts the man with the blaster. "You'll block the shot!"

It is all the opening Ferus needs.

The first man throws a punch. Ferus ducks and grabs his forearm in a durasteel grip. He pulls the struggling man into a tight embrace, using his body as a shield. The blaster bolts stop instantly.

The pain in his head ebbs away, and the moment stretches. He is suddenly clear on how to end this.

The Force is with him again.

Ferus grabs the thug he's using as a shield and flings him toward the man holding the blaster. It is a direct hit. They stumble backward and hit the ground in a tangled heap. The blaster goes flying. Ferus lunges forward and snatches it out of the air. He grips his lightsaber, poised to strike.

But the men stay on the ground. They know this is over.

"I don't want to hurt you," Ferus growls, as the thugs cower beneath him. He suddenly realizes this is a lie. They are enemies of the princess — thus he wants to destroy them.

It is a dangerous emotion, and he allows it to flow through him, leaking away. He has seen what anger can do. It offers a sweet power that he never wants to taste again.

Only one of the men is still on his feet, and he takes a step toward Ferus, then thinks better of it. Ferus gestures to the ground with his lightsaber. The man drops down beside his fellow conspirators.

Ferus feels a tinge of battle rush, the dizzy excitement that always follows a victory. It's been so long since he has stood against an enemy face to face. So long since he's gripped his lightsaber with anything but nostalgia and regret.

His lightsaber . . . They have not seen his face, but they have seen his weapon. If stories spread of a Jedi wandering the streets of Alderaan, it will draw the Empire's scrutiny. He has endangered himself. Which means he has endangered Leia.

Vader would kill them, *Ferus thinks suddenly. They are my enemies, they are Leia's enemies. Vader would argue that it is the only way.*

There was a time when dark thoughts like that bubbled up inside of him, disguised as his own. The dark side of the Force lay at the bottom of a steep cliff, and he had come far too close to the edge.

Those days are behind him.

He reaches out with the Force, shaping their minds to his will. "You wish to leave this planet," he says without malice. "Leave the system. You no longer wish to work for Senator Aak, or anyone who would use a child as a bargaining chip."

The men shake their heads, their gazes blank. "We wish to leave this planet," they chorus.

"No one attacked you tonight," Ferus says, retreating into the night. "There was no Jedi. No lightsaber. You never even saw the princess."

One of the men elbows another. "Let's get out of here," he says, sounding confused. "What are we doing, helping some political hack use a kid as a bargaining chip?"

"Not just the planet," another of the men says. "Let's get out of the system."

"Why are we even out here tonight?" the third says, as they wander off into the night.

Ferus still needs to deal with Senator Aak, to make sure this never happens again. That will not be as easy. But for tonight, he has succeeded. The princess is safe.

Ferus thought he had experienced too much grief in his life to ever hurt again.

Wrong.

His body felt wrenched out of shape, the absence of Obi-Wan as visceral as a missing limb. He somehow found enough strength to return to his own chambers, but once there, he was lost.

He had lived with an ever present ache for years, ever since Leia had grown old enough to take her own stand against the Empire. Ferus knew he couldn't follow her to the Galactic Senate, just as he couldn't follow her on Rebel missions. He had found the strength to let her go off on her own, but he had never found a way to make the agonizing worry fade.

Ferus had been in space when Alderaan was attacked. Terrified by reports that Leia's ship had been destroyed, Bail Organa had sent him to investigate. Ferus had long refused to join Organa's Rebel Alliance — however much he may have wanted to fight the Empire, his place was in the shadows. His role was protector, not warrior. But this wasn't about the Alliance, this was about helping Leia, and it was a request Organa knew Ferus would never refuse.

It was a request that had saved him. Shortly after Ferus lifted off, Alderaan had been destroyed. That same day, reports had surfaced that the princess was safe and sound. Knowing that Leia was safe had offered Ferus his only consolation in the time of unthinkable tragedy.

It had never occurred to him that Leia wasn't the only one to worry about.

Like all Padawans at the Jedi Temple, Ferus had grown up without parents, without a family. But who needed a mother or a father, when you had Jedi Masters like Yoda, Siri Tachi, and Obi-Wan Kenobi shaping your path?

When Ferus had decided to leave the Jedi Order, Obi-Wan had accepted his decision. Years away from the Jedi had not dimmed his respect for the great Master, tempered as it often was by irritation. The deep bond between them rested not only on their shared past, but on their future, and the fact that after Order Sixty-Six, each was all that the other had left.

"Never pause too long to mourn the dead, lest you do disservice to the living."

At the sound of the familiar voice, laced with dry wit and a hint of good humor, Ferus whirled around. And there he was. Well, not *there*, exactly. Not in the full-bodied flesh. Shimmering, translucent, present and yet somehow absent at the same time—but *there*. "Obi-Wan?" Ferus gasped. "But you're—"

"Dead. Yes." Obi-Wan smiled sadly. He seemed older than Ferus remembered, his face ravaged by age. Was it life that had been so hard on him, or death? "A necessary inconvenience."

"How is this possible?"

"The past is the past," Obi-Wan said brusquely. "We have much to discuss about our present dilemmas. First —"

"No!" It was so typical of Obi-Wan, this refusal to offer any "unnecessary" explanation. The Jedi was just as infuriating from beyond the grave. "You expect me to act as if nothing of importance has occurred?"

There was a long silence. "You've suffered greatly, I know," Obi-Wan said finally, his voice grave. "But you are not alone, Ferus." He spoke as if he could see inside Ferus's head.

Maybe he could.

The two men stood silently for several moments, absorbing the emotion of the situation, letting it flow through and between them. This was the Jedi way, to acknowledge, and move on.

Gradually, Ferus pulled himself together, accepting the new reality. As if sensing his ability to continue, Obi-Wan spoke. He told Ferus what had happened to him on Tatooine, how he and Luke had faced Darth Vader on the Death Star . . . how he had fallen.

"It's imperative that Luke not learn the truth about his father," Obi-Wan said urgently. "He's not ready."

"I don't see how I can train him without revealing his past," Ferus argued. "It wouldn't be fair to him."

"You won't be training him," Obi-Wan said. "Luke has learned all he needs to know for the moment, or at least all he can absorb. He needs time."

"What he needs is a lightsaber lesson!" Ferus argued. "Time won't give him control of the Force, or teach him how to fight the battles you know he will face."

"But it will allow him to discover the kind of man he is."

And without our guidance, what kind of man will he be? Ferus thought. *How will we learn whether darkness dwells inside of him?*

But out of respect for the fallen Master, he kept this fear to himself.

"In other words, you want to watch and wait," he said, instead. "As usual."

"The time when I could give you orders is long behind us," Obi-Wan said. "I can only ask that you trust me."

"It would mean keeping my identity from him," Ferus warned. "Allowing him to believe that he's truly alone."

"He's not alone," Obi-Wan pointed out. "He has Leia."

And so they came to the subject Ferus had been hoping to avoid. "And Leia, what of her? You would have me continue to lie to her as well? Let her fight side by side with her brother, never knowing who he is — or what *she* is?"

"You have many secrets from her."

It plagued him. Each morning, Ferus woke up, wondering, *Is this the day? Will I finally reveal everything?* But something always held him back. *She wasn't ready,* he told himself. Not yet.

Now he wondered whether that was caution — or fear. While Luke seemed so youthful and naive, Leia was wise and strong. She was everything that Obi-Wan hoped Luke would become — even if Obi-Wan, so focused on Luke, couldn't see it.

Just like Anakin. Ferus immediately tried to squelch the thought. Obi-Wan had been so determined to see the best in Anakin, so sure that his Padawan was the chosen one, superior to all others. How much had that certainty blinded him to the dangerous reality?

This was different, Ferus told himself. It was understandable that Obi-Wan focused on Luke, even to the point of overlooking Leia's potential. But Ferus had no such excuse. If Obi-Wan had deemed Luke ready for the truth — or part of it, at least — maybe he owed Leia the same.

"Only you know what Leia is capable of, and what she needs," Obi-Wan said. Again, Ferus wondered if the Jedi

Master could penetrate his thoughts. "As I ask for your trust, I give you mine."

Only then did Ferus realize how much he'd been hoping Obi-Wan would tell him what to do. Much as he hated taking orders, this was one decision he'd prefer leaving to someone else.

Hundreds of survivors crowded into the large chamber, their bodies packed together. There was no space large enough for the thousands of Alderaan survivors who would have wanted to attend a memorial. So these six hundred had been drawn by lot. Everyone else would — if they chose — watch a Live Holonet broadcast.

Var Lyonn introduced Leia, then stepped off the podium, joining Han behind the stage. "She's rather magnificent, isn't she?" Lyonn murmured. Han, who didn't trust the man, answered with a terse nod.

But he agreed.

Leia stood before the crowd for several long moments without speaking. Han didn't know how she could stand it, staring out at their miserable faces. He looked away from them, up at the arched ceiling, its ribbons of colored transparisteel showering the room with dancing greens and blues.

"We will never replace what we have lost," Leia said slowly. She spoke softly, but the circling ampdroids carried her voice throughout the chamber. "We can only remember it."

She pressed a button on the podium, and a large viewscreen behind her flickered to life. There, in vibrant, living color, were the Alderaan grass seas. The skies alive with swooping thrantas. The polar sea shimmering with ice.

There were gasps from the audience. A few muffled sobs. And then a solemn silence.

The images were unrelenting: The towering Oro Woods, threaded with glittering rainbow-colored lichen. The imposing Castle Lands, casting their solemn shadow over the surrounding plains. As a lost world flickered behind her, Leia spoke of the beauty of Alderaan and those who lived there. She spoke of the lives lost, never once mentioning the losses she'd personally suffered. That was something she never spoke of, Han had noticed. Publicly, at least, she mourned the destruction of Alderaan as its sovereign — never as a fellow citizen who had lost her family and her home.

"Upon this stage is an empty capsule," Leia told the crowd. "And now I ask you, each of you, to fill it. With your memories and your keepsakes, with gifts for the ones you lost, with symbols and reminders of what you miss the most. There is a home here for each of your memories. And when this capsule is sealed, it will be jettisoned into space. Into the debris field that exists where there should be a planet. I'm told that some call it the Graveyard, but I choose to believe that Alderaan lives on there, not in space, but in spirit. This capsule will do what all of us long to do, and never can. It will return home."

There was a pause, so silent and still that it seemed the room had stopped breathing. And then a young woman in the front row climbed onto the stage. She paused before the empty capsule, her lips moving soundlessly. Then she dropped a small, polished stone inside. Soon she was surrounded by survivors, eager to put something of their own in the capsule. They had come prepared. One by one, perfectly orderly, with frowns and sorry smiles and tears streaming, they filed past. Crowding the stage, the capsule, and when it was over, Leia. Their princess.

Han couldn't stand it. All this raw emotion — it wasn't his thing. "Keep an eye on her, will ya?" he asked Chewbacca, who barked a *yes*. Han slipped outside, threading through the crowds of those who couldn't fit into the building but still wanted to be near.

Suddenly, Han spotted a familiar-looking mop of greasy hair. He shot out an arm and clamped his hand down on the kid's shoulder. "You!"

It was the punk from the day before, the one who'd tried to scam them out of their credits. His eyes went wide with panic, and he tried to wriggle out of Han's grip, but Han held tight.

The other two boys approached, one obviously terrified, the other doing his best to look fierce. "Let him go," the bolder one ordered.

Han suppressed a grin. "Or what?"

"Or . . . or . . . " He obviously couldn't come up with anything.

It was equally obvious he wasn't about to leave his friend behind. Han couldn't help but admire him, thief or not.

He glared at the kid straining against his grip. "If I let you go, you promise not to disappear on me?"

"He doesn't promise anything," the mouthy one said. "You want to turn us in, go ahead. We're not going to help you."

"Why would I want to turn you in?"

"Why wouldn't you? We tried to steal from you."

The kid may have been bold, but he wasn't very bright, not if he was standing here in public admitting to his crimes. Han could have taught him a few things.

If he was in the business of babysitting bothersome little punks, of course.

"For one thing, you may be thieves, but you're not very good thieves," Han said. He smirked. "And for an *old man*, I know a thing or two about needing to steal."

The kid jerked his head at the one Han was holding onto. The boy immediately stopped squirming. Han let go.

"What do you want?" the boldest one said. "We don't have all day."

Acting like he's in charge, Han thought with a grin. *Kid doesn't know when to keep his mouth shut.*

"I can get you inside," Han offered. "If you want."

The kids shook their heads.

"But you're here," Han said. "You don't want to see the show?"

"Only here because we got nowhere else to be," the lead kid said. He was a bad liar, but Han let it pass.

"Hungry?" he asked. They shook their heads — but when he offered them the bag of Corellian potato sticks he'd been snacking on, they took it.

"So you're from Alderaan?" he asked.

"From nowhere," the kid said. "Not anymore."

"Come on, Mazi, not today," one of the other boys said.

"*Every* day, Jez." The one called Mazi scowled and shoved his hands into his pockets. "You ask me, we're better off forgetting the whole thing ever happened. We *are* from nowhere. Now."

"I can't forget," the third, youngest boy said softly. He kept his eyes on the entrance to the building, as if secretly wishing he could go inside. "I don't want to."

Now that they'd dropped the tough act, Han realized they were younger than he'd thought. The oldest couldn't be more than fifteen, if that. Some might think that was too young to be on your own. Han knew better.

"Go on," Mazi said. "Ask. You know you want to."

Han shrugged. "Maybe I'm like you, kid. I don't want anything."

"He means you can ask us how we ended up here," the smallest one said. "We don't care."

Han did want to know. But not as much, he suspected, as they wanted to tell him. "You got me," he said. "Shoot."

"It was my idea," Mazi said. "Jez and Lan didn't think our parents would agree, but I talked 'em into it."

"Mazi can talk anyone into anything," Lan said, looking at the older boy with something close to worship.

Mazi shrugged, but a smile pulled at the corners of his lips. "Dad was easy. Like always. But Mom . . ."

"She thought we were too young to go by ourselves," Jez said. "She worries a lot."

"Worried," Mazi said sharply.

Jez flinched. "Yeah."

"There was a smashball tournament on Delaya," Mazi said in a dead voice. "We got permission to go to the game, stay overnight on our own, then go back to Alderaan in the morning."

Han winced. "But that was the day . . ."

"Yeah," Mazi snapped. "That was the day. So here we are. On our own." He glared at Han. "Don't think you have to pity us or something. We're fine. We know how to get by. We do what we need to do."

"Yeah," Han said. "I can see that."

"So aren't you going to tell us how everything's going to be okay, blah blah whatever?"

Han pressed his lips together. He leaned back against the wall, tipping his head up to the sky. He'd heard Alderaan had once been close enough that you could see it with the naked eye. Not in the daytime, of course. Under the bright sun it was easy to imagine that Alderaan was still up there somewhere. But Han didn't believe in lying to himself.

He knew what these kids were in for. He'd been there.

"Kid, if you're lucky, you'll live through it. Nothing I can tell you but that."

I've never known her, Luke thought, watching Leia greet the admiring crowds. *Not really.*

Watching her preside over the memorial, watching her now console her subjects, Luke realized that this royal bearing was no act. She was still the same Leia that he'd come to know, but she was more than that: a Senator. A princess. For the first time, Luke understood these weren't just titles — they were a part of her.

"Luke, this is Kiro Chen," she said now, introducing him to a young man with dark hair and a timid smile. Like the other survivors, his eyes were hooded and rimmed by red. Something about him seemed familiar, though Luke was sure they'd never met. They followed her to a secluded area behind the stage. "He's the one I told you about, who's been working with General Rieekan on recruitment efforts. We couldn't have set up tomorrow's meeting without him."

Luke gave him a terse nod. "So did you know?" he asked. "About the warehouses?"

Kiro's eyes widened. "Of course not! Leia just told me, and I'm as horrified as the rest of you."

Luke frowned. "But if you've been here all this time—"

"Drop it, Luke. He's been busy trying to help the Alliance," Leia said, in a tone that defied argument. "You can't blame him for believing Var Lyonn's lies, any more than you can blame me."

It was strange to see Leia so obviously comfortable with a stranger. Usually she was guarded, almost icy, in front of people she didn't know. But obviously Leia trusted this man. *Maybe it's because they're both from Alderaan*, Luke thought. *They share a common pain.*

Kiro was an ally, and Leia's ready trust in him shouldn't have bothered Luke.

But it did.

"So it's true!" Halle Dray appeared beside them, as if out of nowhere. Beside her was J'er Nahj — and Fess Ilee. "You come here claiming to want to help us, but all you really want are more martyrs for your cause."

Leia looked at her. "I don't know what you're talking about."

"There are rumors, Your Highness," Nahj said. His voice was gentler, but contained no kindness. "And given that you're here with *him* —" He glared at Kiro.

"I don't even know you," Kiro said. "Either of you."

"But we know *you*," Halle said. "And we know what you've been up to."

Nahj looked sorrowfully at Leia. "It's hard to avoid the conclusion that you're recruiting soldiers for your Alliance."

"It's not *my* Alliance," Leia said, a little of the old fire returning to her voice. "It fights for all of us."

"Not for me," Halle snapped. "The Alderaan of my youth rejected fighting. It outlawed weapons, turned away from violence — until the blood-thirsty Organa family sucked it into a war it could never win."

"That's not how it happened!" Luke protested.

Halle turned the full power of her glare on him. "Stay out of things that don't concern you," she said in a low, dangerous voice. "Especially when you don't know what you're talking about."

"I know —"

"Luke!" Leia quieted him with a look. "It's fine."

"Her Highness only wants what is best for us," Kiro said. "We're all on the same side here. She's not your enemy."

"Alderaan had no enemies before her," Halle hissed. "Now we have no Alderaan. Call it what you want, but that's no coincidence."

Leia stayed silent. It was unlike her, refusing to defend herself in the face of such an attack.

"The Empire is an enemy to all of us, including Alderaan," Kiro argued. "And it's our duty to fight back."

"Yes, I've heard that's your line," Halle sneered. "I've been looking forward to meeting this Kiro Chen I've heard so much about, the one who delights in leading our people to the slaughter. There's something I've been wanting to say to you."

She slapped his face. Then walked away.

Kiro rubbed his hand across his cheek, where Halle's hand had left an angry red mark. "She's upset," he said, almost to himself. "She doesn't know what she's saying."

"We're all upset," Nahj said. He spoke softly, but his eyes were angry. "When you promised to help us in any way you could, Your Highness, I didn't realize that meant sending us off to die at the hands of the Empire."

"Every Rebel is a *volunteer*," Leia said. "Every man and woman here is free to choose."

Luke shot her a sharp look. She was coming dangerously close to admitting that Halle and Nahj were right, that she was recruiting for the Rebel Alliance. It was a dangerous slip. And that wasn't like her, either.

"You're their leader," Nahj snapped. "They do as you ask."

Their leader, Luke noted, not *our*.

Leia whipped her gaze toward Fess. "Does he speak for you, too?"

"I speak for myself," Fess said.

It was odd. Luke had heard Leia's stories about Fess's buffoonery and empty-headedness. But the stories didn't match the man.

"You take danger upon yourself so easily," Fess said, "and the fight is all you need to sustain you. So it's understandably difficult for you to understand that these people here don't need a fight. They need food. Bacta. Blankets. You're offering them a war. That's no substitute for a home."

"I'm offering them a reason to *live*," Leia shot back. "The Alliance gives me a reason to go forward. Everyone should have that chance."

"Not everyone's like you," Fess pointed out. "Some people just want to live in peace."

Luke flashed back to Uncle Owen and Aunt Beru's broken bodies. They'd never wanted to fight anyone. But the Empire hadn't cared.

"Not everyone's like *you*, either," Leia said, her face white with rage. "Not everyone's so craven and weak. So *useless*."

Fess opened his mouth — then shut it again. He turned to Nahj. "I think it's best if I go."

Nahj nodded. "I'll go with you." He extended a hand to Leia. "You made me a promise, Your Highness. I hope you do not forget it."

"I've promised to defeat the Empire," Leia said. "And nothing's more important than that."

CHAPTER TWELVE

You're late," Halle Dray snarled, barring the door. "You're sure no one followed you?"

Ferus nodded. "Why do you think I'm late?"

She stepped aside.

"You never mentioned you were so cozy with the princess," she said, as he followed her into the abandoned house. The others had already arrived. They were assembled in the dusty remains of the living room. Shards of transparisteel littered the floor, and moonlight filtered in through the shattered windows. It was a sad, forgotten place in a sad, forgotten corner of the city. A perfect spot for secrets.

"Cozy isn't the word I would use," Ferus pointed out. "In case you hadn't noticed, she hates me. Even more so, now that she realizes I'm with you."

"That's right." Halle's voice was laced with sarcasm. "Sometimes I forget — you're with us."

It had taken Ferus very little time to get the others to trust him, but Halle Dray remained the lone holdout. He didn't take it personally: She trusted no one.

J'er Nahj had once told Ferus that she'd worked at a wildlife medcenter on Alderaan, tending to injured stalking birds and sick grazers. But that was *before*, in what she referred to as her other life. If there was any gentleness left in her now, she hid it well.

"We were right," Halle told the group, as the meeting began. "Leia is here to draft survivors into the Rebellion. She pretends to want to help us, but she's just looking for martyrs to her cause."

"Do you have proof?" Ferus asked.

"Wherever Leia goes, a new crop of Rebel fighters is sure to follow. I don't believe in that kind of coincidence."

Ferus frowned. "Leia's Rebel sympathies are well known. It doesn't mean she's on a recruiting mission."

"Wake up, Fess," Halle snapped. "She's had her minions poking around Delaya for weeks now. And here she is to close the deal. You saw her with Kiro Chen."

There was murmuring at the name. Though none of them knew Kiro personally, it was common knowledge that he'd been working with General Rieekan. And everyone knew that Rieekan spoke for the Alliance.

"I wanted to believe that she was sincere about trying to help us," Nahj said. "But it seems clear that she has other priorities."

The twin brothers Driscoll and Trey Bruhnej muttered to each other in disgust. "She hasn't gotten enough of us killed?" Driscoll said aloud.

"Apparently two billion isn't enough to satisfy her," Halle said. "Which is why this time, we're going to stop her."

"And how exactly will we do that?" Ferus asked dryly, concealing his concern.

"Tomorrow night, she and her allies plan to sneak away from their government 'protectors,'" Halle said. "They've planned a secret meeting with those of our people foolish enough to believe their Rebel lies. That meeting is *not* going to happen."

Ferus kept his expression blank. So Halle had someone watching Leia. Against his will, his mind jumped instantly to the boys he occasionally paid to run errands. Mazi and his brothers seemed willing to do just about anything for credits. Had it been mere coincidence that they'd attacked Leia in that alley?

Like Halle, Ferus was reluctant to believe in coincidences.

J'er Nahj shook his head. "Disrupting the meeting won't help. If our people are foolish enough to join the princess and her Rebellion, they will do so — tomorrow or the next day."

"They can't join the princess if the princess is no longer asking," Halle said.

"She won't stop," Nahj said. "She doesn't seem to understand that Alderaan has paid enough."

"Why should she?" Halle scoffed. "When she's paid nothing."

It was far from the truth, Ferus knew. But he stayed silent.

"The meeting won't happen because the princess won't be available," Halle added. "She'll be with us."

"Kidnapping?" Nahj said. "No."

"You disapprove of the methods?" Halle asked wryly. "I admit I'm rather surprised."

"That was a mistake," Nahj protested. "And the boy proved it when he helped us of his own accord."

Ferus suppressed his anger. He'd heard rumors, but this was the first confirmation. So Nahj had taken Luke to the warehouse against his will — and somehow, Luke had turned the situation to his advantage. But if things had gone wrong . . .

It was terrifying, how fragile the situation was. If Obi-Wan was right about Luke, and the future of the galaxy rested on his shoulders, how could it be right to let him blunder around without proper training and protection? What if the unthinkable happened?

"That may have been a mistake," Halle said, "but this isn't. Princess Leia is a valuable commodity — rumor is the Emperor himself wants to get his hands on her. Just imagine what he might be willing to offer us in return."

"You're talking about ransoming off the princess? To the *Empire?*" Nahj asked in disbelief. "They'd kill her."

"They'd give us a home," Halle said quietly. "A new planet. A new Alderaan."

"What makes you think that?" Driscoll asked.

"Because they've already agreed."

"You contacted the Empire?" Ferus asked. Nausea swept over him at the thought of Darth Vader's ship hurtling toward the planet, his dark shadow creeping over Leia . . .

"Halle, how could you?" Nahj asked.

"Look what she's done to us!" Halle cried fiercely. "Alderaan is *gone* and still she longs for more death. Our troubles won't end until someone stops her. And if, in doing so, we gain a new home for ourselves? Can't you see it, J'er? The sacrifice of one — for the good of so many." She slapped her palms flat against the table. "The Empire is only our enemy because the princess *made* them our enemy. We were a peaceful people, once, and the Empire understands that we can be peaceful again. They want to help us . . . if we help them."

"You've been planning this for a while," Nahj guessed.

"We knew Leia would show up eventually," Halle said, unashamed. "I intended to be ready."

Driscoll and Trey gave each other a long, intense look, as if exchanging some kind of silent twin communication. They nodded as one. "Yes. We agree."

Halle looked at Nahj. "I don't like it either, J'er," she said quietly. "If there were another way . . ."

Nahj lowered his eyes. "Yes, if there were another way . . . but perhaps there is not."

Fess couldn't believe it. Nahj was passionate about what he believed in, but had always seemed kind and reasonable. How could he — how could any of them — convince himself that this was right?

"And you, Fess?" Halle said, turning the name into a hiss. "You're awfully quiet. If you disapprove, feel free to leave right now."

Ferus knew that if he objected, there was a slim chance he might sway them. Explain to them how it felt to compromise yourself to evil, bit by bit, until there was no turning back. On the other hand, if he failed to convince them, they would cut him off. He wouldn't learn the details of their plan; he would lose his chance to save Leia.

From the beginning, he'd sensed that this group could prove dangerous. And Halle's fierce hatred of Leia had concerned him. He'd suspected that if there was trouble, Leia could end up in the middle of it. This was why he'd worked so hard to worm his way in. It seemed foolish to walk away now, just when his efforts were paying off.

He'd made so many wrong decisions in his life.

What was one more?

"I'm in."

Luke was almost relieved when he heard the knock. He'd spent the last hour pacing restlessly, listening to Kiro Chen and Leia strategize. He didn't feel that it was his place to express any opinions — even Han was keeping his mouth shut. But it was more than a little frustrating to stand silent.

Not that Luke disagreed with everything Leia said. The success of the Rebellion was crucial. Beating the Empire *mattered*. He was just no longer sure it was *all* that mattered. But Leia didn't want to hear that, not from him. She'd made that perfectly clear.

Any distraction would be a welcome one.

He opened the door and took a step backward. Fess Ilee stared back at him. Luke didn't know what it was about the man that made him feel comfortable and unnerved, both at the same time. He stepped aside, allowing Fess into the room.

"Your Highness, we have a problem," Fess said abruptly.

Leia arched an eyebrow. "*We?*"

"Greetings, sir," C-3PO interrupted, eager to finally observe some protocol. "Might I offer you a drink, or perhaps some fresh-baked sweesonberry loaf?"

"He's not staying," Leia said sharply.

"I've come only to bring a message, and then I'll go," Fess said.

"Well? I'm listening."

Fess looked around the crowded room, the suspicion clear in his eyes.

"Everyone in this room has proven their loyalty to the cause," Leia said. "Except you."

Fess looked doubtful, but he gave in. "You can't attend your meeting tomorrow. You're in danger."

Leia cast a sharp glance at Kiro. "What meeting?" she asked innocently.

Fess shook his head. "There's no time for that now. I know about the meeting you're planning for tomorrow — and so do Halle Dray and J'er Nahj. They're planning to grab you and hand you over to the Empire."

"I've spoken with Nahj, and he seemed like a good man," Leia said skeptically. "I can't believe he would resort to kidnapping."

Luke winced. "I believe he would, Leia." As he told them the truth of how he'd first met J'er Nahj, Luke felt a sharp stab of guilt. His lie to Leia had nearly put her in danger.

Leia was looking at him curiously, like she wanted to ask why he'd kept this a secret until now. But she didn't. Maybe she just thought he'd lie to her all over again.

Instead, she turned to Fess. "Why come to me with this? You've made it very clear that you're against us."

"I'm with anyone who stands up to the Empire," Fess admitted. "Halle and Nahj mean well, but they tend to act rashly. I let them believe I agreed with them because I thought it might be the only way to stop them from doing something they can't take back. I see I was right."

"Except you weren't able to stop them," Leia pointed out. "So you've come here, to stop us, instead. I won't run away. I came here to find reinforcements for the Rebel fight, and that's what I'm going to do."

"Even if it gets you killed?" Han asked sourly. "Last time you messed with the Empire, they weren't exactly rolling out the royal welcome wagon."

Luke hated to agree with him, but . . .

"You're too important to the Alliance," he said. "We can't risk your safety."

"We can't risk the *galaxy*," Leia shot back.

"Might I suggest a compromise, princess Leia?" Kiro said hesitantly. "Simply move the meeting to a different time and location."

"And what's to stop one of the leaders you're meeting from reporting the new plans back to Nahj?" Fess asked. "You may have got a leak."

"So we give them a false rendezvous point," Kiro said. "When they arrive, we'll confiscate their comlinks, then lead them to the princess. That way, they have no chance to report her coordinates to anyone."

"I think you're forgetting our biggest problem," Han cut in. "We can handle this amateur stuff—but the Imperials are on their way. Am I the only one who'd rather be someplace else when they arrive?"

"Sounds like the Empire is expecting Halle and Nahj to do their dirty work for them," Kiro argued. "You can spend the night on your ship—it's safer there, anyway. We meet first thing in the morning. You'll be off-planet by the time Nahj and his group know what happened."

"Risky, but it could work," Elad said.

"I don't know," Luke said, watching Kiro closely. It felt wrong to discuss Leia's safety with outsiders in the room. "It sounds dangerous."

"Since when are *you* afraid of a little danger?" Leia asked.

"This is different," Luke said fiercely.

"Why?"

Because this is you. But he knew better than to say it out loud.

The night is alive with shadows. Leia can feel them out there, watching her, following her. She wants to go home.

But the streets all look the same. She is walking in circles. Lost.

The palace sits on a wide stretch of ground, its towers climbing high into the sky. She should be able to see it in the distance — but the buildings block her view. She needs to get to high ground.

She comes upon a half-finished building, a thin durasteel crane climbing up its stories of scaffolding. This is her answer. She scrambles onto the mast of the crane, propelling herself up its rungs. It's easy, like climbing a ladder, and soon she is ten stories above the ground. The arm of the crane overhangs a narrow catwalk that wraps around the unfinished building. She climbs onto it, slowly circling the scaffolding, staring out at the city. Your *city*, her father always tells her. Someday, it will be your responsibility.

The city twinkles beneath her, and she can see the lights of the palace off to the east.

She knows the way home.

Eagerly, she climbs down. Too eagerly.

Her foot skids off a rung.

Her fingers slip.

She is falling.

She reaches out but her hands clutch nothing but air. The rushing wind is icy against her face. For a moment, time seems to stretch out. She notices the moonlight *glimmering off the durasteel. The stars twinkling over-head. The strange freedom of the fall, her legs and arms flailing through empty air, her stomach in her throat. And then the world speeds up again, and the ground, an unfor-giving plane of duracrete, once so far away, is hurtling toward her. She screams, but the wind snatches the shriek out of her mouth and carries it away, and the ground is closer, and she is —*

Caught.

For a moment, she thinks her father has saved her. But it is not her father lowering her to the ground. It is the detestable Fess Ilee.

She jerks away from him and dusts herself off.

"What are you doing here?" she asks, her heart still pounding. She looks up to the top of the crane — up and up — wondering what would have happened if he hadn't caught her.

I would have caught myself, *she thinks angrily.* But he didn't give me the chance.

"I've come to take you home, Leia," he says.

She crosses her arms. "I don't need you," she spits out. "I can do it myself. I know how to go."

He nods. "Then you lead the way."

She walks east. She doesn't look back. Fess makes no noise, but she knows he is following. A small piece of her is glad. This only makes her hate him more.

The walk is long, her legs tired. As night leaks into day, she can barely keep her eyes open. She sits for a moment to rest, and lets her eyes drift shut. Only for a moment.

The next thing she knows, someone is carrying her. "Father?" she murmurs, still half asleep.

"It's just Fess," he says.

She wants to tell him that she doesn't need him, that she can do it herself. But she is so tired.

"Don't worry, you're safe with me."

She yawns, and closes her eyes again. "I know."

CHAPTER THIRTEEN

You sure about this?" Luke asked nervously, glancing at Kiro Chen.

"He's sure," Leia snapped.

Leia had put out the word that the Rebel recruiting meeting had been rescheduled, and would take place in one of the T'iil Blossom Homes. But when the attendees arrived, they would find only Luke and Han, ready to confiscate their comlinks and lead them to the real location. Kiro and Leia would be waiting.

"At least let me send Chewie with you," Han said, sounding tense. Luke wondered if he was worried, too.

Kiro shook his head. A thin rivulet of sweat trickled down his neck. "The Wookiee would draw attention. But if you don't trust me to protect you, Your Highness, perhaps you would feel more secure if one of your friends accompanied us."

"No," Leia said fiercely. "How many times do I need to tell you all that I can protect myself."

"I know that," Luke said. "But . . ."

"But what?"

Luke just shook his head in frustration. They'd argued all night long, and Leia hadn't budged. She was holding this meeting, no matter what. And she wanted Kiro Chen by her side when it happened. "He's one of us," she'd told Luke, Han, and Elad.

The unspoken meaning was clear: *He's one of us. You're not.*

"Don't worry," Kiro assured Luke. "Everything's going to go as planned. Easy as skinning a nerf."

Luke looked at him for a long moment, once again seized by the certainty that he'd met Kiro somewhere before. The answer dangled almost within reach — and then was gone.

Han, Luke, and Chewbacca traipsed silently through the Delayan streets. They were nearly empty this time of morning, giving the city a sad air of abandonment. A few times, passing a dark window or shadowed entryway, Luke thought he caught a pair of eyes watching him. But whenever he turned to look, they were gone.

"I'll be glad to get off this rock," Han grumbled. Chewbacca barked his agreement.

"So why'd you stick around in the first place?" Luke asked.

Han shrugged. "Couldn't tell ya, kid. It just felt wrong to leave her here alone —"

"She's not *alone*," Luke said indignantly. "I'm here."

"Yeah, and so's that blasted protocol droid of yours, but when the trouble starts, he's not exactly the guy you want in your corner."

"I can protect her just as well as you can," Luke protested. "Better, even."

"Whatever you say, kid." Han shook his head. "Besides, it's not like she wants either one of us to protect her.

"What makes you think we'll have anything to protect her from?" Luke asked. "It's a good plan." But he could feel it, too. Something dark, hovering at the fringes of his mind.

Han groaned. "Where've you been, kid? Something *always* goes wrong." He rolled his eyes. "But listen to that Kiro character and you'd think we were taking a trip to the Galactic Fair. 'Easy as skinning a nerf.' Right."

Luke stopped walking so abruptly that Chewbacca slammed into him, nearly knocking him to the ground. Han caught his arm and yanked him upright.

"Say that again," Luke said, as the darkness he'd been sensing began to take shape.

"Say what again? 'Easy as skinning a nerf?'"

Luke gasped. "It's him!"

"Him who?"

Chewbacca roared in confusion.

"I don't *know* what he's talking about," Han snapped. "That's what I'm trying to find out!"

But there wasn't time to explain. Leia was in danger. He took off running back toward the hotel. "It's Kiro Chen!" he shouted over his shoulder, as Han and Chewbacca raced after him. "He's not who he says he is!"

Easy as skinning a nerf.

Now he knew why Kiro had seemed familiar. It wasn't his face — it was his *voice*. The same voice he'd heard outside J'er Nahj's lean-to the first day they'd met, arguing with Halle Dray about whether the young boy should have to apologize to Luke.

Kiro had claimed he didn't know Halle, or Nahj. He'd lied. Who knew what else he'd lied about — or what else he wanted?

And now he was alone with Leia.

Exactly as he'd planned.

Han spotted them first, arguing on a street corner. Kiro was tugging at Leia's arm, but she'd planted her feet firmly and crossed her arms. Finally, her stubbornness was coming in handy.

Han pulled Luke to a stop, pointing toward the princess. If they approached calmly, without revealing that they knew something was up, there was still a chance to —

"Leia!" Luke shouted, waving his arms at the princess. "Get away from him!"

"Great work, kid," Han muttered under his breath. He pulled out his blaster and started running again. This was about to get messy.

Leia backed away from Kiro, who pulled out a blaster of his own, aiming it at the princess. She froze.

"Careful," Kiro said, as Luke, Han, and Chewbacca approached. "I don't want to hurt her."

"Then how 'bout you drop the blaster!" Han shouted.

"Don't upset him," Luke murmured.

"Me?" Han shot back, out of the corner of his mouth. "*You're* telling *me* to stay calm, after what you —"

The kid looked more clueless than usual.

"Ah, forget it." Han turned his attention back to Kiro and Leia. She had her hands up, and was glaring at Kiro. Han cocked his blaster, but kept it aimed at the ground.

"You want to protect her?" Kiro asked, sounding almost sorry. "Drop your weapons."

Han caught Leia's eye. She gave him an imperceptible nod. He grinned, his grip tightening on the blaster. "I would, but last I heard, her highness prefers to protect herself!"

He raised his weapon. Kiro swung around to face Han, firing off a round of laser bolts. Han ducked the blasts, reluctant to fire back with Leia still in range.

But the princess could take care of herself. Taking advantage of Kiro's distraction, Leia dropped to a crouch. She rolled toward Kiro and knocked his legs out from under him. His blaster clattered to the ground. They lunged for it at the same time.

"Out of the way, Leia!" Han shouted. "I can't get a clear shot."

Leia and Kiro wrestled for the blaster. Kiro's finger brushed the hilt, but Leia grabbed his wrist just in time, twisting it behind his back. He grunted in pain, shrugging her off with surprising strength. She tumbled backward, but managed to kick the blaster out of his reach as she fell. Then she slammed into the ground, hard. Kiro scrabbled forward and snatched the weapon.

"Leia, go!" Han shouted, taking aim. She climbed to her feet and took a few steps, then, collapsed back to the ground, clutching her ankle. Her face twisted in pain.

Han jerked his head at Luke. "Get her *out* of there." Luke was already on his way.

Kiro wheeled toward her, his blaster raised, but Chewbacca threw himself in the line of fire. The Wookiee barreled toward Kiro. Grunting with effort, Leia forced herself to her feet and began a limping run. But before Luke could reach her, two figures melted out of the shadow, blasters aimed at his head. He hesitated, giving them the chance they needed to close in on Leia. One of them kept his blaster aimed at Luke, while the other lunged at Leia, jabbing an injector syringe into her shoulder. She lashed out, sinking her fist into his stomach — then sank into his arms with a small sigh.

"Leia!" Han shouted in alarm.

Chewbacca, who had been twisting Kiro into a knot, dropped the man and rushed to help the princess. Using Leia as a shield, the men backed away. One of them raised a comlink to his lips. "Now!" he snapped.

A large speeder truck whooshed down the street, screeching to a halt just long enough for the men to toss Leia inside and hop in after her. They scooped up Kiro's limp body and sped away. Han took aim — but didn't shoot. He couldn't risk causing a crash — not with Leia inside.

The speeder disappeared around a corner.

Luke sank to his knees. "I let her go," he said, sounding dazed. He unclipped the lightsaber from his belt. "If I'd trusted myself enough to use it . . ."

"Then you'd probably have gotten yourself killed, kid," Han said impatiently. They were wasting time. "At least you're still in one piece. That'll come in handy when we rescue her."

"She trusted me," Luke said, as if Han hadn't spoken. "I was supposed to protect her."

Han ran out of patience. "So do it!" he snapped. "She's out there somewhere, counting on us to find her."

Luke stood up, and retrieved his blaster. "You're right," he said, with renewed determination. "Let's find her."

Chewbacca growled the question that Han had been trying to avoid.

"I don't *know* how," Han retorted. "But we *will*."

He had to.

I was supposed to protect her, Luke had said, blaming himself.

But you weren't, kid, Han thought, watching Luke take a few practice swipes with his lightsaber, as if the weapon were good for anything but party tricks. *That was my job.*

The Alderaanians were running out of patience. As the minutes passed, they gathered around Ferus, clamoring for answers.

"You said she'd be here!"

"What kind of game is this?"

"Is this all a big joke to you?"

But Ferus had nothing to give them beyond empty reassurances. He'd been expecting Han and Luke more than twenty minutes ago. Something had obviously gone wrong. But until he received details, there was nothing he could do.

His comlink signaled an incoming transmission.

"It's me," Halle Dray's voice said. "Where are you?"

Ferus stepped away from the crowd. "In my room," Ferus lied. "Getting ready for tonight." He knew Halle and her group still thought the meeting was going on as planned. Apparently their leak was less reliable than they'd thought. "What do you need?"

"I just wanted you to hear it from me."

"Hear what?"

There was a pause, a jumble of voices in the background, and then:

"What am I supposed to say?" Leia's voice.

"That'll do quite nicely," Halle said.

A poisonous brew of rage and fear began churning in Ferus's gut. "You have the princess," he said, keeping his emotions under tight control. "Congratulations. I thought we weren't moving until tonight."

"And Nahj thought 'we' included *you*," Halle said coldly. "I suspected differently. I see that I was right."

"You set me up," Ferus said, the pieces beginning to fall into place. "You told me about your plans—"

"To see if you'd go running straight to the princess. Which you did." Halle laughed harshly. "Job well done."

She broke the connection.

"Was that the princess?" someone asked. "Is she on her way?"

Ferus couldn't answer.

He'd done it yet again—failed the person he most wanted to protect. And it could have been avoided, had he only paid attention. He'd devoted all his energy to the big picture, getting swept up in questions of Luke and Leia's parentage, their future, the fate of the Empire. He'd lost track of the present, and missed crucial details. If he'd been listening to the Force, he would have heard what was approaching.

But he'd listened to nothing but the drumbeat of his fears for Leia, and he'd let that thunder drown out everything else.

Not again, Ferus vowed to himself—to Leia. He'd lost too much.

He wouldn't lose her too.

Ferus has never felt such a moment of perfect fear. He sees the princess at the top of the crane, seeming so much smaller from so far away. She swings herself onto the catwalk with an easy grace, and he admires the way she fearlessly tiptoes across. Her instincts and reflexes are beyond human. She is strong with the Force, even stronger than he had expected.

But she is untrained, and as she scrambles down the scaffolding, he sees her hand slip. Her foot misses its grip. She lets out an alarmed squeal and begins to slide—

Ferus moves with lightning speed, nearly flying up the side of the scaffolding. He catches her.

She is angry; she resents his help. But he will not leave her behind, not again. And by the time they are halfway home, she is asleep in his arms.

He walks slowly, carefully cradling the snoring bundle in his arms. He has not held her like this since she was a toddler. On the day he first came to Bail Organa to explain his mission, Organa had placed Leia in his arms.

Ferus had put her down immediately. How could he remain objective if he let emotions cloud his judgment? The Jedi way repudiated attachments, even to a small child — perhaps especially to a small child. He had turned from that way once, and the consequences had been cata-strophic. Never again, *he thought.*

Now he knows he has been a fool.

He has denied the truth — and this, too, is not the Jedi way.

Leia is not a job. She is a child. And he loves her like she is his own.

He has been arguing with Obi-Wan about whether to begin training the Skywalker children as Jedi. Obi-Wan, as always, urges caution. Ferus has his doubts. Shouldn't Luke and Leia be given the chance to explore their gift, to protect themselves?

Doesn't the galaxy deserve a new generation of champions?

"That's what they have us for," Obi-Wan always says. "Until they're older. Until things change."

Until the Emperor is not ruthlessly seeking out and murdering all Force-sensitive children, he means. Until teaching them the ways of the Force is not a death sentence.

And, the thought that is on both their minds, though neither will speak it aloud: Until we are sure they will not be like their father.

Looking down at Leia, Ferus now understands he will argue no more. Leia might be the key to defeating the Empire — but for now, she is a little girl. Ferus knows he will not risk her safety for anything. Not for the Force, not for the fate of the galaxy. He will save her from the truth about herself, until he knows she is strong enough to survive it. He will always save her.

Nothing matters more than that.

he woke up in the back of a large speeder truck, her wrists and ankles bound. J'er Nahj leaned over her, dabbing a drop of blood off her forehead.

"Good," he said softly. "You're all right."

"Hardly," Leia said dryly, struggling into a sitting position.

A man she'd never seen before was at the controls. Kiro Chen lay on a seat just behind him, his head on Halle Dray's lap, his eyes closed. Halle chewed on her lower lip and stroked his hair, never taking her eyes off his face.

Leia was on the floor of the speeder, just behind them, propped up against the back door. If she could find a way to open it and slip out . . .

"Not a good idea," Nahj said. "At the speed we're going, you'd be killed before you hit the ground. Just sit tight, Your Highness. You'll be all right."

"Don't waste your breath," Halle said. "She's not worth it. Look what her friends did to Kiro!"

"They were just defending themselves," Nahj pointed out. "He'll be fine."

Halle whirled around to glare at Leia. "He better be."

"He wouldn't be here right now if he hadn't betrayed me," Leia pointed out. She realized this plan must have been a long time in the making. Had Kiro been planning it from the beginning, when he first contacted General Rieekan? Had it all been a trap, designed to snare her? And she'd walked right into it, blind to the possibility that one of her own people could betray her.

"No, he wouldn't be here right now if *you* hadn't betrayed *us*," Halle snapped. "None of us would. You put these events in motion, princess. Whatever happens next, just remember that."

"Nothing's going to happen," Nahj said. "We won't harm you."

"Don't act like you feel sorry for her! After all the pain she's caused?"

I've done nothing wrong! But Leia couldn't say the words out loud.

Beside her, Kiro stirred. "Don't," he murmured.

"It's okay," Halle said, in a soft voice that made her sound like a different person. "They can't hurt you anymore."

"No, I mean, don't yell at her like that. She means well."

Halle shook her head. "You're confused. You don't know what you're saying."

Kiro sat up, shooting Leia an apologetic look. "I'm not confused."

"So you're taking her side now?" Halle asked. "You want to call it off?"

Kiro hesitated, then put an arm around Halle. "No, this is the right move. I trust you on that. But there's no reason to make it harder than it has to be."

Leia's heart thudded. "Make *what* harder?"

"Look at it this way," Halle replied. "You claim you'd do anything to help the survivors of Alderaan?"

"It's not a *claim*," Leia shot back. "It's the truth."

"Then you should be happy to sacrifice yourself for the greater good."

X-7 was finally alone. Leia's bumbling friends had split up to search for her. X-7 had volunteered to cozy up to Prime Minister Manaa and Deputy Minister Var Lyonn, in case they knew anything. But helping Leia was of no concern to him. All his efforts to break through her guard had proven useless. Maybe with her out of the way, the others would be more forthcoming.

It had been a calculated risk, supporting the princess in her ridiculous plan. Pretending not to see that her new friend Kiro Chen was deceiving her. But his instincts had told him to go along with it, and X-7 relied on them without question. It had been infuriating, watching Chen weasel his way in, gaining her trust with such ease. The only consolation was that X-7 hadn't been the only one shut out. There was no question that the time on Delaya had driven a wedge between Leia and her friends. X-7 had stayed in the background, silent and accepting, in hopes that when the princess turned to someone, she would turn to him. Events hadn't played out in the way he had expected, yet X-7 still expected to turn the situation to his advantage.

If the others found her in time, he would lead the rescue and burrow even deeper into her favor.

If she died, there would be chaos. And when people were panicked, grief-stricken, and confused, it was child's play to get them to do whatever you wanted.

Either way, X-7 had no interest in leading the search. Pretending to be a normal human with normal human emotion was exhausting. And the more he tired himself, the greater chance there was he would make a fatal error.

This was the perfect opportunity for a break.

But just as he was settling into his blissfully blank repose, his comlink activated with an incoming transmission over the secure line. It was the Commander.

"Are you aware that Princess Leia has been kidnapped, and that her captors have plans to hand her over to the Empire?" he asked.

X-7 nodded.

The Commander's face flushed an angry red. "And are you aware that this has all happened at the command of *the Dark One*?"

Everyone knew it was unsafe to speak Darth Vader's name, even over an encrypted channel. But the Commander's meaning was clear.

"I was not aware."

The Commander bared his teeth in the predatory grimace of a rancor ready to strike. "Are you aware that the Dark One has made it a top priority to track down the pilot who destroyed the Death Star? That he might be on his way to Delaya as we speak, to personally supervise the interrogation?"

"I was not aware."

The Commander's rage exploded. "*Are you aware of anything, you bantha-brained bludfly?*"

X-7 swallowed hard.

"You will find Leia before his men can interrogate her," the Commander ordered. "*You* will interrogate her, and you will find the answers we seek. Enough delay! Get the job done, X-7. Or suffer the consequences."

No one at the warehouses would speak to them. At least, not about J'er Nahj, Halle Dray, or Kiro Chen. Leia was merely an outsider. Princess of a planet that no longer existed. Neither Luke nor Han could convince them of anything else.

Fess had come up empty as well. He'd checked all the meeting spots used by Nahj and Halle's group, but there was no sign of any of them.

"You couldn't have known," Luke kept assuring him. "This isn't your fault." Fess didn't seem convinced.

"It's not your fault either, kid," Han reminded Luke. Han suspected he was blaming himself for keeping quiet about Nahj's little kidnapping habit. Sure, he'd made a mistake trusting Nahj. But then, Han had made a mistake trusting Kiro Chen. They all had. And now Leia was paying for it.

Leia had been gone for three hours, and they were no closer to finding her.

They were trudging through a narrow alley on their way back to their quarters when Han stopped abruptly.

"What?" Luke asked. Han shushed him, listening hard. Fess caught his eye and nodded. He'd heard it, too. Fess pointed toward a side alley that led to a dead end. Han led them in, giving Chewbacca a silent signal to hang back. Luke looked confused, but he followed along.

They'd made it almost to the end of the alley when Han spun around, his blaster raised and ready to fire. "You want to come out, whoever you are?"

Nothing happened.

Chewbacca positioned himself at the other end of the alley, blocking the way of anyone who might try to escape.

"We don't have time for this," Luke complained.

"He's there," Fess said with an odd certainty. "You've got nothing to fear from us!"

Han rolled his eyes. That wasn't exactly the message he would have sent to a shadowy figure following him into a dark alley. But it had become clear the old man liked to do things his own way. Han played along, lowering the blaster. "Yeah, come on out, or stop wasting my time."

There was a flicker of movement behind one of the towering piles of garbage. It was the kid, Mazi. This time, he was alone.

Han sighed. He didn't have time to play babysitter.

"You know something," Fess said. It wasn't a question.

Mazi shrugged. "Hear you been looking around for Halle."

"You know where she is?" Luke asked.

Mazi shrugged again.

"Tell us!" Luke shouted.

125

Fess shot Luke a sharp glance.

"Let me handle this," Han said. He tapped the pocket where he kept his credits. "How much you want, kid?"

"Didn't come here looking for a payday," Mazi mumbled.

"Then what?" Again, Han wondered how long this kid would last on the streets. Rule number one: Someone offers you cash, you take it.

Mazi shifted his weight. "I met Princess Leia once, you know? School trip to the palace. Dead boring. But she was nice and all."

"Nice, huh?" Han grinned. "Not the first word that comes to mind."

"There's this place Halle and Kiro go when they want to be alone," Mazi said. "This abandoned schoolhouse, a few blocks up the river. They think it's like this big romantic secret or something that they're together. Usually pretend they don't even know each other."

"So how come you know?" Han asked.

"I know a lot of stuff," Mazi said. "It's easy to be invisible, when you want to be."

"And sometimes when you don't," Han said quietly.

"Whatever. Anyway, that's all I got." He turned to leave.

"Wait." Han pulled out a handful of credits.

"I told you, I didn't come here for that."

Han shoved the money into his hand. "Just take it, kid."

Mazi grabbed the credits and ran off.

"What are you all looking at?" Han asked, realizing Fess and Luke were staring at him.

"You were rather good with him, Captain Solo," Fess said. "I wouldn't have guessed."

Chewbacca barked in agreement.

"He just reminds me of someone," Han mumbled. He brushed past the others, heading out of the alley. "Now can we stop wasting time and go find Leia?"

They charged down the street, seeking out the building that Mazi had described. "Stay strong, your highness," Han heard Fess murmur. "We're on our way."

CHAPTER FIFTEEN

tay strong, your highness. We're on our way.

It wasn't a voice in her head. It was just a feeling, a moment of calm and confidence. As if Luke was there with her, lending her some of that infuriating certainty that right would prevail. She stared blankly at the wall of her dim cell, trying to picture Luke's face.

But it wasn't Luke's face she saw, it was Fess's.

"You're sure we can trust them?" Nahj's voice carried through the narrow gap between the ceiling and the door.

"We're not giving them the prisoner until we get evidence that they're serious about resettlement," Halle said.

"Unless they decide to come and *take* her," Nahj pointed out.

"The Empire doesn't know where we're holding her," Kiro said. "Halle thought of everything."

"The man I've been dealing with reports directly to his Lordship Darth Vader," Halle boasted. "This is a done deal. You know Vader has the authority to make it happen."

"I've heard he can make *anything* happen," Nahj muttered. "That's what concerns me."

Whatever brief spurt of confidence Leia had felt was gone. All with a single word: *Vader.* She'd faced him before, and that was enough for one lifetime. If her friends really were coming to rescue her, they'd better hurry.

So you're just going to sit around and wait, Your Highness? Giving up that easy?

This time, the voice was in her head — cool, mocking, and completely her imagination.

I didn't realize you were such a pushover, Your Majesty. She could almost picture Han's crooked smile, goading her on. *I know you royal folk are used to having everything done for you, so this may come as a surprise: Some of us rescue ourselves.*

And, as so often happened when faced with Han's gundark-headed taunts, she couldn't help herself. She smiled.

Who's giving up? she asked the imaginary Han.

Halle Dray had told her she deserved this. That if she truly loved Alderaan, she'd be willing to give her life for its revival.

Whatever I've done, it's not Halle Dray's job to punish me, Leia thought. Sacrificing herself to the Emperor was no way to honor the billions who'd died at his hand.

She'd barely looked at her cell, but now she scrutinized it, her mind racing, frantically searching for options. The room was only four or five meters wide, with four blank walls and a single locked durasteel door. The cheap flooring tiles sagged beneath her. The floor bulged in one corner, the plasteel tiles peeling up at the edges as if something lay beneath.

Leia got on her hands and knees and dug her fingers into one of the peeling tiles, trying to pry it up. She grunted in pain as two of her nails broke off, but she kept scrabbling at the scuffed plasteel.

The tile popped off. The one next to it lifted off easily, and the next, and the next, until Leia had uncovered a narrow grate over a dark shaft. Some kind of old heating vent, perhaps, or an air duct.

Or an escape route. Leia unscrewed the grate and eased herself into the opening. It was just large enough for her to squeeze through. She didn't pause to consider where the dark tunnel might lead — it was away from the cell. And for now, that would have to be enough.

The air shaft was dank and slimy. Leia dropped down several meters, landing hard as the shaft flattened out.

She slithered on her stomach as the shaft sagged beneath her weight. It was holding . . . for now.

The shaft began to climb. As it grew steeper, Leia braced her feet against its sides to keep herself from sliding backward. She inched up the slope, using her legs to push herself forward. It was grueling and maddeningly slow — and then, abruptly, the shaft leveled off again. Light filtered up through a grate, illuminating the wall that lay before her. She'd hit a dead end.

The grate lifted off easily. Leia peered through the opening. She looked down — way down — on a wide, empty room, scattered with piles of durasteel girders and abandoned scaffolding. Her captors must have brought her to one of the abandoned construction sites scattering the city. Now she was suspended at least thirty meters above a duracrete floor.

A thin crane climbed toward the ceiling, several meters below and to the left. If she could propel herself from the grate at just the right angle, with enough momentum, she might be able to grab it. *Might.*

And then, if she didn't miss her grip and go plummeting to her death, she might be able to climb down.

Might.

Leia lowered herself down, feet first, holding so tight to the edge that her knuckles turned white. Then she began to swing her legs back and forth, building up momentum.

Scared, Your Worship? Han's voice taunted, as she hesitated. *Maybe if you wait long enough, someone will build you a royal turbolift.*

Get out of my head! Leia silently shouted and, with a deep breath, swung herself forward and let go.

For a moment, she was flying, arms outstretched.

She slammed into the crane. Her head thudded against the durasteel with a dull clang. She could taste blood dripping from a split lip. But she was alive.

Leia wrapped her arms around the crane, hugging it to her chest, her feet scrabbling for purchase. *One miracle down*, she thought, trying not to look at the all-too-distant ground. *One to go.*

She felt no fear. There was something familiar about the cold durasteel of the crane against her skin, the dizzying height. Thin ridges jutted out at regular intervals along the mast of the crane, and she was able to climb down without much difficulty — until she got overconfident. The next foothold she reached for wasn't there, her fingers slipped their grip, and suddenly she was hurtling toward the ground.

Instinct took over. Her arm shot out, grabbing for the scaffolding at the exact moment it flew past. She made contact. Her shoulder nearly tore out of its socket, but she held on, dangling by one arm, fifteen meters above the ground. A narrow catwalk stretched above her. She need only pull herself up and climb down.

Unbelievable, she thought in wonder. Grabbing hold of that scaffolding at the right instant had been an incredibly lucky one-in-a-hundred shot.

And then the bar from which she hung gave out. As it snapped free of the scaffolding, she reached desperately for the edge of the catwalk. She caught herself just in time, hanging by her fingertips. But the bar tumbled to the floor, crashing into a pile of durasteel girders with an echoing clang that seemed to shake the building.

She heard a shout, then footsteps, running toward her.

With the last of her strength, Leia swung herself up onto the catwalk. But it was too late. But the time she'd regained her footing, Halle's men had arrived. Three of them, blasters aimed.

"Get her down from there," Halle ordered her men. "Then bring her back with us so we can keep an eye on her. Just in case she's stupid enough to try this again."

Sorry about all this," Kiro murmured, as he fastened her restraints. Leia pretended not to hear.

Halle Dray stood before her, clapping slowly. "Impressive," she jeered. "Not what I would have expected from a coddled member of the royal family."

Leia glared at her captor. "My father never coddled me," she said in an even voice. "He showed me how to stand on my own. To *fight*."

Halle perched on the edge of a durasteel girder, bringing her face level with Leia's. "Yes, your father knew plenty about fighting, didn't he? Alderaan was a peace-loving planet, but that wasn't good enough for him, was it? He needed the glory of battle. Even if it meant turning his planet into an enemy of the Empire. Even if it meant destroying us all."

Enough. Let them accuse her all they wanted — but there was no way Leia would let them attack her father.

"My father *loved* Alderaan," she snarled.

Halle shook her head. "No. He loved the glory of war."

It was Leia who had first urged her father to join the Rebellion. Leia who had fought for Alderaan to take up arms after so many years of peace. *Will you be the one to bring war to us?* he had once asked.

But in the end, he had agreed.

"The people of Alderaan believed in my father," Leia insisted.

"'The people,' taken as a whole, are almost always reckless and stupid," Halle snapped. "You and your father preyed on their foolishness. You re-armed a planet that had turned its back on violence. You linked it with the Rebel Alliance. And you — yes, *you*, Princess Leia — you gave the Emperor the final excuse he needed."

Leia heard Grand Moff Tarkin's voice, as she heard it in her nightmares. *In a way, you have determined the choice of the planet that will be destroyed first.*

"No!" she shouted. Halle could blather on as much as she wanted. But Leia needed to silence the voice in her head. "I'm proud of everything I've done. Can you — any of you — say the same?"

Kiro and Nahj both looked away, shame tingeing their expressions. But Halle was uncowed. "I've done only what I need to do. Sacrifices are always necessary for the greater good."

"No good can come of cooperating with the Empire," Leia protested. She turned her gaze toward Kiro. He'd been working on behalf of the Alliance for weeks — yes, it had all been an act, but he seemed so apologetic now. Wasn't there a chance that some small part of him believed in her? If she could persuade him . . . "The Empire is *evil*, you must see that after what they've done. There can be no good in the galaxy until the Empire is destroyed. This is why we fight. Why we *must* fight."

Kiro cleared his throat. "Halle, maybe . . ."

"Kiro, get my medpac and find something to tend to the prisoner's wounds," Halle ordered. "I'm sure Vader's men expect to find her in good condition."

"But —"

"Kiro, now!" Halle snapped. Then she drew in a slow breath, calming herself. She stood up, grasping his wrists and bringing her face close to his. "You know this is right," she said in a low voice. "I need you to believe in me."

Kiro hesitated, his eyes darting to Leia. Then he gave Halle a soft kiss on the forehead. "Always," he promised her.

There was a storage area off to Leia's right. Halle waited for Kiro to disappear through the door before she spoke again.

"Don't you *dare* try to use him against me," Halle warned Leia. "He'll never betray me."

Ignoring the pain, Leia drew her bloodied lips back in the approximation of a smile. "Some people will do whatever's necessary for the greater good."

"Halle, they're here!" J'er Nahj cried, before she could respond. Four Imperial stormtroopers clomped toward them, their heavy boots slapping the floor in lockstep. Behind them appeared a slim, gray-haired man.

Halle flipped open her comlink. "Driscoll, you were supposed to alert me if the Imperials arrived. Driscoll? Trey? Hello?" No response.

"I'm afraid your friends have other things to worry about," the man said. "You'd best worry about yourself. Halle Dray, I assume?"

She nodded. "How did you find us?"

"That's my job," the officer said. "No one can hide from the Empire."

Halle didn't flinch. "Have you brought the plans for the New Alderaan resettlement?"

The Imperial officer shook his head.

"The terms of our agreement were that you would get the prisoner only once the Empire begins relocating the refugees."

"The terms have been changed." He signaled the stormtroopers. As one, they raised their blasters and fired.

The laserbolts struck Halle Dray and J'er Nahj at the same moment. Both were direct hits.

It seemed like their bodies collapsed to the floor in slow motion. Leia forced herself not to look away. *Remember this,* she ordered herself, staring hard at their limp, pale limbs, at the scorch marks across their chests. At their sightless eyes, wide open, gazing blankly into the void. *Remember every life the Empire has taken.*

Halle and Nahj had been her captors. But they had also been her people.

Remember — then avenge.

"There's supposed to be a third," the Imperial said, kicking each of the bodies to make sure they were dead. "*Find* him."

Leia glanced toward the storage area, and saw Kiro's eyes peering out of the darkness. He was at her mercy.

"The third one ran off shortly before you arrived," she told the Imperial. "The sniveling coward couldn't take the pressure."

He raised his eyebrows. "Your help in the matter is rather unexpected, princess."

"You and I may be on opposite sides," Leia said, trying to sound as cold and unfeeling as him. "But we certainly agree that this scum deserves to die."

The Imperial nodded to the stormtroopers. "TB-278, TB-137, see if you can track him down. TB-31 and TB-2954, take her back to the temporary base and see she's prepared for interrogation. I'll alert Lord Vader of our progress." He swept his eyes across her body, staring so intently it was almost like he could see inside of her. She forced herself not to cringe. "I doubt I'll be seeing you again, your highness. Not alive, at least."

He spun on his heel and walked away.

As the stormtroopers carried her from the room, she arched her head back, and saw Kiro poke his head out of the shadows. He took a step toward her, a question on his face. Leia gave her head a slight shake. *Run,* she mouthed.

He hesitated, his eyes wide and anguished. *Run!* she urged him again.

He couldn't save her. But he could save himself. And no matter what he'd done, he was still one of her subjects. Which meant he was her responsibility.

Kiro nodded, once, then slipped back into the shadows. As the stormtroopers carried her away, she felt a faint whisper of relief.

At least one of us will escape.

CHAPTER
SEVENTEEN

There's no one here," Luke said, once they'd conducted a cursory search of the hollowed-out school building. Its rust red paint was peeling off the walls, and crushed transparisteel glittered on the floor. A few tattered drawings still fluttered on the wall, leftovers from an unimaginable past. It had taken them far too long to track down the building. And now, after all that wasted time, there was nothing. "Let's go — maybe Han found something in the other wing."

He's too impatient, Ferus thought. *So eager to move onto the next thing that he misses what's right in front of him.* It wasn't untypical for a Padawan, but then, Luke wasn't a Padawan. He had no Master to show him a better way.

He could have me.

"Wait," Ferus said, stretching out with the Force. They were not alone.

"Wait for *what*?" Luke asked, annoyed. "You stay if you want. I'm leaving."

That's when Ferus heard it. A distant, muffled moaning. "Come on." Ferus hurried toward the source of the sound, without bothering to see if Luke would follow. He crept into one of the empty classrooms, crossing to a desk in the back of the room. Kiro Chen lay curled up underneath, hugging his arms to his chest. Weeping.

Ferus touched the man's shoulder. He didn't react. "Kiro."

Kiro looked up at him with blank, wild eyes. "They killed her! They killed her, and I didn't know where else to go. It wasn't supposed to be this way."

Surely I would know if she was dead, Ferus assured himself. *I would sense it.*

"Leia?" Luke said, his voice cracking on the name. "They killed Leia?"

Kiro shuddered, and buried his face in his hands. "I loved her. It wasn't supposed to be this way. It wasn't."

"Halle?" Ferus guessed softly. Regret mixed with relief.

Kiro groaned. "Dead."

Ferus took Kiro by the shoulders and, gently, pulled him out from under the desk. Kiro didn't resist as Ferus guided him to a chair.

"Tell us where they are," Luke urged him. "Where did you take Leia?"

Tears streamed down Kiro's face. "I lost everyone. Everything. And then I found her — and they took her from me, too."

Ferus nodded. "It is a tragic loss, Kiro, and I'm sorry —"

"*Sorry*?" Luke repeated incredulously. "He kidnapped Leia. And now he's the only one who knows where to find her." He grabbed Kiro by the shoulders, shaking him roughly. "Where is she? *Where?*"

Kiro choked on his sobs, sucking in air like he couldn't get enough to breathe.

"Answer me!" Luke shouted.

There's so much anger in him, Ferus thought.

Luke's hand strayed toward his lightsaber.

Enough, Ferus thought in alarm. He grabbed Luke's wrist. "No," he said firmly. "This is not the way."

Rage filled Luke's eyes and, for a moment, Ferus feared he was about to strike. But instead, he dropped his arm back to his side. "I wasn't going to hurt him."

"I know," Ferus assured him.

This was a lie.

"He knows where she is," Luke said desperately. "He knows, and he won't tell us."

"Because he can't tell us. Not like this." Ferus knelt by Kiro's side, placing a comforting hand on the man's shoulder. Kiro shuddered beneath his touch. "Anger is never the answer," he told Luke. "Whatever you gain from it never makes up for what you lose."

Luke nodded.

But does he really understand? Ferus thought. *Or is he just pretending, the way Anakin used to? Biding his time?*

Ferus reminded himself that these were extreme circumstances. He understood Luke's desperation, because he shared it.

He shut his doubts out of his mind and let the Force flow through him. He didn't suppress his fear, he embraced it, accepted it as a necessary reaction to events, then let it go. He imagined himself as the eye of the storm, peaceful and serene, then let that calm flow through his body and into Kiro Chen. "Your loss has been great, my friend. Your sorrow beyond measure," he said soothingly, letting his voice rise and fall like the lapping river. The words weren't as important as the emotion they carried. Ferus could sense that Kiro was a good man. He wanted to help. But he was locked inside his grief. "You think your life is empty. Frozen, because how can it move forward? How can it survive this? How can *you*?"

As he spoke, Ferus allowed himself to remember all the losses he'd tried too hard to forget. The names and faces who haunted his nightmares. "But you *did* survive," he said. "And by accepting that, you honor her sacrifice."

"It wasn't her fault," Kiro said. "She did what she thought was right. I tried to talk her out of it, but she never listened to anyone. She was always so certain, and this time . . ."

"If you don't help us, more will die," Ferus said quietly. "Princess Leia will die."

Kiro took a deep, shuddering breath. "I don't know where the Imperials took her."

Ferus exchanged a glance with Luke. The same hopeless frustration was painted across both their faces.

Until Kiro spoke again. "But I know someone who will."

Deputy Minister Var Lyonn liked to work late. And he liked to work alone. It meant he could focus on his tasks without any distractions. It also meant that when two men blasted through his office door, then aimed their weapons at his head, there was no one to hear him scream.

He screamed quite a bit.

"Give it a rest," Han snapped. Time was running out. And he was getting a headache. "We're not here to kill you."

Lyonn reached for a switch on the corner of his desk. A laserbolt shot across the room, blowing a hole in the expensive wood. Lyonn yanked his hand back. "No need to call in reinforcements," Fess said calmly. "You'll be gone by the time they get here."

"And just where am I going?" Lyonn said, trying and failing to sound like he was in control of himself or anything else.

"You're going to take us to wherever the Empire has stashed the princess."

Var Lyonn went white. "The princess is . . . missing?"

"She is," Fess said. "Thanks in part to you."

"I don't know what you're talking about."

Another laserbolt whizzed by, this one blasting a hole in the wall just behind Lyonn's left ear. "Try again," Fess growled.

"You can't blame me!" Var Lyonn squeaked. "I had to do what was best for Delaya! We have enough problems of our own, without all these survivors sapping our resources. The Empire promised to help!"

"In return for giving them Leia." Han was glad that they'd agreed Fess would do all the blasting. Han would have been too tempted to blow a hole straight through this skrag. "So you did it. And now you're going to help us get her back."

There were no Imperial guards posted outside the deserted medcenter, but the place had a sinister feel. Maybe it was the boarded up windows, or the sentry droids hovering at the perimeter, but Han was certain this was the place.

You only needed to look at Var Lyonn to know he'd told the truth. He stood at the lone entrance of the medcenter, legs trembling, sweat bleeding through his shirt. He banged on the door again. "Let me in!" he shouted in a high, quivering voice.

"Stop shaking!" Han hissed from his hiding place in the bushes. "If they suspect you've betrayed them, they'll kill you."

"Is that supposed to make him feel *better*?" Luke asked.

Fess shushed them both.

With the addition of Elad, there were five of them. Although Luke was still hit-or-miss with a blaster, and the old man was . . . well, an old man. Then there were the droids, who Han refused to count at all. If Lyonn could get them inside, it just might be enough — or not. They had no idea how many Imperials they were facing, or where Leia was being held. More time might have allowed them to make a better plan.

But who knew how much time Leia had left?

The door slid open. Two stormtroopers stood in the entrance.

"Just a few more steps, fellas," Han muttered, waiting impatiently for a clear shot. Lyonn was supposed to get the guards to step out of the building. Han and Luke would take them down, then don their armor. Dressed as stormtroopers, they'd infiltrate the facility, find the princess, and get her out. It was a crazy plan — but it had worked before.

Mostly.

"I need to see your lieutenant," Lyonn said loudly. Then he leaned toward the stormtroopers, saying something Han was too far away to hear.

"Blast it!" Han swore. "I knew this would happen."

"What?" Luke asked, just as one of the stormtroopers raised his comlink. The other raised a blaster, taking aim for the bushes.

"Go!" Han shouted. They scattered. A barrage of laserbolts slammed into the foliage, sending billowing plumes of dirt into the air. Han darted through the cloud, firing at one of the stormtroopers. He went down.

"Watch out!" Luke shouted, knocking Han out of the way just in time to avoid another laserbolt which whizzed past.

Chewbacca roared, charging the door with his Ryk blade held high. The stormtrooper fired wildly, sending a blast straight into Var Lyonn, who shrieked and dropped to the ground. Before the stormtrooper could reload, Chewbacca had grabbed his blaster and twisted it out of his hands — then he set to work twisting the stormtrooper.

"Oh dear, Artoo, where do you think you're going?" C-3PO cried from his hiding spot. But the little astro-mech droid ignored him, rolling steadily toward the door. He positioned himself in its path, just as it was slid-ing shut.

C-3PO dodged the laserbolts flying all around him to join his stubborn counterpart. "You simply must get out of there," he insisted. "You're a droid, not a doorstop."

R2-D2 beeped indignantly.

"Why I'm most certainly doing something to help," C-3PO protested. "I'm offering my opinion on how things should proceed." He turned toward the battle, shaking his golden arms in the air. "Uh, I suggest you shoot at that stormtrooper, Captain Solo. Oh, dear, Master Luke, you might want to get out of the way!"

"Stop wasting my time and let's go find the princess!" Han shouted, knocking out the last stormtrooper. The melted, carbon-scored plasteel armor would be no use as a disguise now. But that likely didn't matter, since the stormtroopers had called for reinforcements. They'd lost the element of surprise.

He vaulted over R2-D2 and sailed through the open door. "Good job, little guy," he called back to the droid, as the others hurtled through the opening.

"Why, thank you, sir," C-3PO answered for both of them. "We live to serve."

"Find the nearest computer terminal," Han ordered the droids. "See if you can get some information for us." But he didn't have much hope. If the Imperials were just using this as a temporary base, there was little chance they'd upload the location of their prisoner into the computer system. Still, he'd try anything. He could already hear the drumbeat of armored boots thudding down the hall, straight for them. Things were about to get very dangerous, very fast.

They strapped her to a flat slab of durasteel. Leia didn't struggle — she didn't want to waste her strength. She suspected she would need everything she had for what was to come.

She had been tortured before, and survived.

Even if there were moments when, torn apart by the pain, she'd wished that she hadn't.

Stun cuffs pinned her wrists and ankles to the durasteel. The stormtroopers snapped another set of binders across her chest, her waist, and her neck. She was completely immobilized.

No fear, she reminded herself.

Whatever they did to her, she would never betray the Rebel Alliance. *Never*.

Once she was immobilized, the stormtroopers marched out, their feet pounding the floor in unison. She was left in a silence broken only by her ragged breathing.

Then, footsteps. A Pau'an, with a gaunt, gray face, clawed hands, and a long black robe. He smiled. "A pleasure to make your acquaintance, Princess Leia."

She spit in his face.

The Pau'an jerked away, swiping the gob of saliva away with the back of his hand. She allowed herself a small moment of satisfaction.

"You'll tell me what I want to know, princess," the Pau'an said in a pinched voice.

"I'm surprised to see a Pau'an working for the Emperor," Leia replied calmly, as if they were having a polite chat. "Given that he's turned your world into a planet of Imperial slaves."

"Not slaves, Your Highness," the alien hissed. "Willing servants of our Imperial masters. True, the Emperor prefers to fill out his ranks with human officers . . . but some of you humans tend to get rather squeamish about torture. Whereas I'll do anything to get the information I desire. And, just between you and me — I'll enjoy it."

The binder restraining her neck was tight enough that she couldn't turn her head. So she closed her eyes. Rough thumbs pressed against her lids, dragging them open. "Look at me," he ordered.

As if she had a choice.

"First: The name of the pilot who destroyed the Death Star. Next: Everything you know about the Rebel Alliance. *Everything.*"

"I'm not telling you anything, scum," Leia spit out. "Do whatever you want. You can't make me talk."

"Incorrect." The Pau'an pulled a thick black handle out of his cloak. A thin strand of wire dangled from one end; he brushed it across her face. "Have you ever seen a neuronic whip, princess? With the press of a switch, a high voltage charge of electricity will shoot through this wire — and into anything it touches."

He glided the whip across her cheekbone . . . down her jawline . . . his finger straying toward the activation switch. Leia tried not to flinch. "One lash is enough to cause debilitating pain, neurological overload. Repeated lashings usually result in permanent brain damage. Very useful on my planet for keeping the slaves in line."

"I thought you said they were willing servants," Leia said through gritted teeth.

"At a certain point, one is *willing* to do anything to make the pain stop," he said coldly. "Do you know much about pain, princess?"

More than you can imagine, you Imperial slime.

He bared his teeth, and moved the whip beyond her field of vision. A moment later, she felt the cold wire brush her neck. "So many kinds of pain." He traced invisible designs in her skin. "Infinite variations." She forced herself not to shiver as the wire ran across her forehead, her temple, over her lips, along her chin. If he activated the charge . . .

"How much pain can you handle?" he asked "How much before you break?"

"I'll never break," she snapped. *No fear*, she told herself again. It should have helped, the knowledge that she'd been tortured before and knew what was coming. She'd carved out a dark, quiet space for herself in the corner of her mind, and curled up until the pain disappeared. But even when the pain had gone, it hadn't been easy to find her way out again. If she had to retreat into the shadows once again, would she ever find her way back?

Still: "Do what you want," she said coldly. "You'll get nothing from me."

"I know," he said abruptly, dropping the whip. It clattered to the floor. "You'll break," he said. "Everyone breaks. Even the strongest have their limits. It's only a matter of how much. Pain will destroy you — either your body, or your mind. I could hurt you, princess." He leaned over her face, his breath misting her forehead. "I could hurt you quite efficiently."

He let out a hissing sigh of irritation. "But I've seen your file. You'd die before you talked — or the pain would drive you to madness, trapping you inside your head forever. You'd be of no use to us then. Fortunately, I've been provided with a third option."

Once again, he held something over her face for her to see. An injector. "One dose of this, and you'll tell me anything I want to know," he boasted. "It bores holes in your brain, burrowing straight through all those troublesome little walls you've erected around the truth. No more secrets, princess. Not from me, and not from the Empire."

Now Leia knew that she hadn't been afraid before, not really.

Because this was fear. Ice pulsing through her veins. Not for herself, not for her own life — but for the Alliance. If the Empire could get inside her brain, they could learn anything.

Names. Bases. Access codes.

All her friends would be in danger, their hopes destroyed.

All because of her. Again.

"Look on the bright side," he said, smirking down at her. "The serum is in the experimental stage — we're still refining the formula."

So maybe it won't work, Leia thought desperately.

"Oh, it gets the job done," the Pau'an said pleasantly. "But only one of our test subjects has survived. She's doing a lot better these days — at least according to the poor sap we pay to mop up her drool. I'm told soon she might even be allowed to feed herself again, if they can teach her to stop stabbing herself in the face with the fork." He shrugged. "Either way, once we're done here, I doubt you'll be in any position to feel guilty about the secrets you've revealed."

Leia felt herself beginning to crumble. She'd always believed she could fight anything.

But what if she couldn't fight this?

I'm sorry, she said silently, to all the men and women she'd promised to protect. To the survivors on Delaya. To the Rebel Alliance. To Luke, to Han. To her father.

To Alderaan.

"Ready?" The Pau'an drew the injector and pressed it to the back of her neck.

But before he could inject her, an alarm ripped through the silence.

His comlink blared. "Intruders!" the tinny voice announced. "Institute emergency protocol!"

The man scowled, laying the injector next to Leia's body. "I'll be back, Your Highness."

"Back from the dead?" Leia snarled, drawing strength from the blaring alarm. Someone had come for her. She wasn't the kind of woman who liked to be rescued.

But it was far better than the alternative.

Ferus dodged a laser blast and threw himself across the hall, slamming into the stormtrooper. He jerked his blaster over his head, smashing it into the trooper's plastoid face plate. With the help of the Force, the blow sent the stormtrooper reeling. Ferus waited for a clear shot, then fired.

His Jedi training gave him an advantage over the enemy. His senses were honed, his motions carefully chosen and lightning quick. As he battled through the crush of stormtroopers, time slowed for him. The Force alerted him when the enemy was set to strike. He darted out of the way an instant before the laserfire could hit its mark, and fought with an acrobatic grace.

Still, he was clumsy with a blaster. With his lightsaber, he could likely have taken out the stormtroopers all on his own. What was the point of keeping his identity a secret if it got them all killed?

Luke wasn't using his lightsaber either, Ferus noted. The boy was good with a blaster, but his hand kept straying to the lightsaber's hilt, as if he were resisting the temptation to activate it.

He's afraid of failure, Ferus thought. *He's afraid to try.*

They battled their way down a long hallway, leaving a trail of armored bodies behind them. Ahead of them, the hall branched off in two directions. More stormtroopers approached from behind.

"Chewie, you search that hall, Luke and I'll take this one," Han shouted, signaling for Elad and Ferus to cover them as they rounded the corner.

Two was almost more effective than five in the narrow hallway. Elad seemed to anticipate Ferus's motions, ducking and weaving out of the way, his shots perfectly timed with Ferus's. *He fights like a Jedi*, Ferus thought.

The stormtroopers surged forward, their boots pounding the ground in lockstep. The air blazed with laser fire. "This isn't working," Elad shouted over the noise. "We need to push back."

Ferus got his meaning. The stormtroopers were advancing toward the end of the hallway — any further, and they'd be able to turn the corner and take off after Han and Luke. He and Elad would have to force them back down to the other end of the hall, and hold them there as long as possible.

Ferus knew he could pull out his lightsaber and dispatch the guards within minutes. But if there was any other way . . .

"In there!" Ferus said suddenly, jerked his head toward one of the open doors along the corridor.

"Run and hide?" Elad asked in disgust, dodging another blast. The hallways was filling up with a smoke so thick they could barely see the enemy.

"Neither," Ferus shot back. He pointed at the large cart just inside the storage closet, piled with medical equipment. Elad glanced over, eyebrows raised. Then he nodded, and darted inside. The stormtroopers fell back as Ferus peppered the hallway with laserfire. He drew on the Force to guide his aim, and the stormtroopers dropped, one by one. But there were still too many of them.

"Ready?" Elad said, pulling the cart out of the closet.

Ferus climbed on top, shifting his balance as Elad began to push. The cart gained momentum, plowing toward the stormtroopers.

They couldn't hit a moving target. Especially one towering several feet over their heads, speeding down the hallway right for them. Ferus bounced on the balls of his feet, trying to maintain his balance as the cart hurtled down the hallway, straight into the ranks of the enemy. The high vantage point gave him a perfect shot. Blast after blast hit its mark, until the corridor was littered with armored bodies. Shielded by the cart, Elad took down his fair share of stormtroopers, blasting with one hand as he pushed Ferus down the hall. He seemed to be shooting blindly, and yet nearly every blast made contact.

Soon only three stormtroopers were still standing. "Retreat!" one of them ordered. In unison, they darted to the edges of the corridor, sheltering themselves behind a series of open doors. Every few seconds, one would peek out just long enough to spray the hall with laserfire then duck back to safety.

Ferus hopped off the cart, feeling a surge of relief. Two against twenty had been daunting odds. Two against three? Even a Padawan could handle that.

But the thought of Padawans made him think of Luke and Leia, and he remembered they were still no closer to rescuing the princess than they'd been before. The relief vanished.

"Cover me," Elad suddenly shouted, dropping to the floor over the body of a fallen stormtrooper. Ferus stood over him, blasting away at the stormtroopers who were left.

Elad ripped off the stormtrooper's armor and dug his fingers into the man's shoulder. He shrieked with pain.

It was a hand-to-hand combat tactic Ferus had never tried: a precise compression of the parascapular nerve that caused unbearable pain. The rare maneuver had been perfected centuries before, but Ferus had seen it performed only once, by an Imperial officer trying to torture information out of a spice smuggler. The officer's expression had been no more single-mindedly brutal than Tobin Elad's.

This is different, Ferus told himself, trying to block out the stormtrooper's agonized cries. *Our cause is just. We have no choice.*

But another, fainter voice drifted through his troubled mind, resonating with Jedi-like assurance. *There is always a choice.*

"Where is the prisoner?" Elad asked. The stormtrooper just screamed. Ferus winced as the man's pain rippled through the Force. Elad just pressed harder. *"Where is she?"*

"Hallway on the right," the stormtrooper moaned. "Third door down."

"That better be the truth," Elad warned him. "Because if she's not there, I'm coming back for you. My friend here is going to leave you alive for me."

"It's true!" the stormtrooper screamed, writhing in pain. "I swear!"

"Enough!" Ferus shouted. "I'll hold them off—you go find Leia. *Go!*"

Elad didn't hesitate. He took off down the hallway.

Ferus activated his lightsaber, and advanced toward the remaining stormtroopers. When they saw he'd dropped the blaster, they abandoned their hiding places and rushed him. Time slowed to a crawl. He struck out with the lightsaber, once, twice, thrusting its glowing blade into the nearest stormtrooper. He somersaulted through the air, dodging the man's fallen body, and deflected a blast of laserfire. The blue beam swooped and swirled, carving elaborate arcs through the air.

A Jedi never craves violence, never enjoys it.

But Ferus's lightsaber had sat hidden and unused for a long time. Wielding it again, finally taking *action* instead of just sitting around and endlessly watching, waiting . . . it felt like coming home.

X-7 raced down the hall, pausing to look back just before he turned the corner. Out of curiosity, not concern. Was the fool already dead?

Two bodies lay on the floor, both of them stormtroopers. And between the two still on their feet, was Fess. But a different Fess than X-7 had seen before. He was leaping nimbly away from the blaster shots, with a dancer's liquid grace. He moved so fast that he almost seemed to be in two or three places at once.

But that wasn't the strangest thing.

The strangest thing was the glowing blue blade slashing through the air, deflecting laserbolts, spiraling toward the stormtroopers and effortlessly slicing through their armor.

So Fess, whoever he was, had a lightsaber. A carefully hidden lightsaber. And, unlike Luke, he seemed to know how to use it.

Interesting.

But not relevant. X-7 filed the information away for later use. He rushed down the hallway. As he neared the third door down, a gaunt, gray alien approached from the other end of the hallway. He drew an oddly shaped weapon from his cloak, some kind of whip. X-7 simply blasted a hole through his head. Then, stepping over the dead body, Elad busted through the door.

"Elad!" Leia cried in relief. "Get me out of here! Before he comes back!"

X-7 took in the durasteel slab, the small table of torture devices, the injector sitting by her head. "What was he going to do to you?"

Leia shuddered in her restraints. "It's some kind of experimental brain agent," she said in disgust. "Designed to wring all the information out of my brain and then destroy it."

X-7 turned his back on the princess and scoured the floor. He seized a twisted piece of metal lying in the corner. He slammed the door shut, then wedged the metal underneath. He'd broken the lock, but this should hold, at least for a few minutes.

"What are you doing?" Leia asked.

He approached the slab. "The building's filled with stormtroopers," he said, peering down at her. She was completely helpless. "Have to keep them out until we're done here."

"Done with what?"

"Getting you out of these restraints," X-7 said, pretending to look around for something to slice through the durasteel. He had to handle this carefully. She'd been tortured before, and resisted. There was a chance that even the mental agent would fail if she tried to fight it.

Which meant he needed to convince her not to fight.

X-7 palmed the injector, then bent over the cuff pinning her left arm to the table, as if examining the locking mechanism. He pulled out his blaster, switching it to the lowest setting, and pressed it to the cuff. "This could hurt, just a bit," he warned her.

She pressed her lips together, steeling herself.

With one hand, he shot the blaster, careful to miss the cuff and lightly singe her skin. With the other, he pressed the injector to her arm and injected the drug. The pain of the blaster bolt would disguise the lesser pain of the injection.

She grimaced. "That didn't feel like it worked."

"Sorry, princess. The binders are stronger than I thought. There must be something in here that will cut them."

"Just hurry," she urged him. "We need to . . ."

"What?" he asked, pretending to search the lab, while keeping a close eye on her. She was breathing rapidly, and her skin had gone pale.

"Nothing, I just feel . . . strange," she said faintly. "Lightheaded."

"You've been through an ordeal," he told her. "It's only natural."

The drug was taking effect. He had to get his answers now, before the others showed up. Or before it killed her. "The Empire went to a lot of trouble to get its hands on you," he said casually.

"I'll never tell them anything," she said. Her eyes fluttered. "I'd die first."

"It must be a burden, keeping all those secrets."

"Is it very hot in here?" she asked, drawing in deep, ragged breaths. "We have to get out of here. Why don't you get me out of these binders?"

"I'm trying," he lied.

"Can't you shoot out the locking mechanism with your blaster?"

He looked at her curiously. "I just tried that," he reminded her. "You don't remember?"

"Of course I remember," she snapped. "I . . ." She shook her head as much as the neck restraint allowed, as if trying to clear the fog. "I'm just so tired."

It was now or never.

"Of course you're tired, Leia," he said kindly, switching on the miniature holorecorder hidden in his utility belt. The Commander would want proof. "You've done everything you could to protect the Rebel Alliance. Especially the pilot who destroyed the Death Star."

"The Empire can never find out who he is," she murmured, sweat beading along her forehead. Her pupils had narrowed to black pinpricks. "We have to protect him."

"I'd lay down my life for him," X-7 said. "But I can only protect him if I know his name."

Her eyes rolled back in her head.

"*Leia!*" he snapped.

A small sigh escaped from her lips.

"His *name*, Leia," X-7 urged her. "Who must we protect? Who destroyed the Death Star?"

"Luke." She smiled. "It was Luke."

Exactly as he had suspected. It would be so easy now to kill her — and then open the door and kill Luke, too. Mission accomplished.

But the Commander had given him strict orders. Learn the name of the pilot and report back. He couldn't act until he got the kill order.

X-7 injected the remains of the serum into her arm. Given what he knew of brain agents, the odds were high that she wouldn't remember any of this when she recovered. If she recovered at all.

"If something happens . . . you have to take care of Luke," she whispered as her eyes slipped shut.

"Oh, don't worry, Your Highness. I will."

Ferus gathered his strength and pushed out with the Force. The door flew open.

Elad stood inside, staring down at a body.

The princess's body.

Elad met Ferus's eyes. "I was too late."

Han, Luke, and Chewbacca burst into the room, freezing alongside Ferus as they caught sight of Leia. Han's voice was ragged. "Is she —"

"No," Ferus and Luke spoke together. Ferus glanced at the boy. So he was connected enough to the Force — or at least to Leia — that he could sense her still pulsing with life.

However faintly.

"Whatever they did to her, she's still alive," Elad confirmed, "but we have to get her out of here." He had already broken through the restraints pinning her to the table.

Ferus scooped Leia off the table and cradled her gently against his chest. She stirred in his arms, her eyelids flickering. "Father?" she mumbled.

"No," he said softly, hurrying toward the exit. The others covered him. They'd taken out all the Imperials, but you never knew when reinforcements would arrive. "It's just —" He hesitated, not wanting to say: *It's Fess.* Not wanting to lie any more. "It's me. Don't worry, you're safe with me."

She smiled, and her eyes drifted shut again. "I know."

CHAPTER TWENTY

Leia hesitated just outside the door to the abandoned schoolhouse. Then she gave herself a little shake, and stepped inside. Luke and Kiro Chen sat side by side, their heads bent together in low conversation.

She cleared her throat.

Luke looked up. "I thought we still had time," he said.

While Fess and Elad had gotten Leia safely out of the medcenter, Han and Luke had ransacked the Imperials' com system. They'd confirmed that there had been no distress call — as far as the Empire was concerned, everything had proceeded as planned. But according to the transmission archives, those plans called for Darth Vader to arrive the next day.

It seemed prudent to blast off the planet before he showed up.

"We do," Leia said. "I just wanted to talk to Kiro before we left." *Wanted*, that was wrong. *Needed*.

Luke stood up. "I'll leave."

"No." She'd had enough of being left alone. "Stay. You're part of this now, too."

Leia sat down across from Kiro. He wouldn't look at her.

"I'm sorry about Halle Dray," she told him. "I know you two were close." Her memories of the kidnapping were strangely fuzzy, as if she'd taken a blow to the head. She remembered little of what had happened after the stormtroopers had taken her away. But she remembered seeing Halle and J'er Nahj hit the ground.

"*I'm* sorry," Kiro said, still keeping his eyes averted. "You should hate me."

"Whatever you did, you did it because you loved Alderaan. I could never hate you for that." Leia paused. "What will you do now?"

"Now?" he looked blank, like he couldn't imagine a future.

"Kiro knows he honors her memory by moving forward," Luke said, encouraging him. "By helping others, the way she wanted to."

Leia frowned. Halle Dray hadn't seemed the type to help anyone. But Kiro had obviously known a different side of her. Or maybe he'd just seen what he wanted to see. "The Rebel Alliance would welcome you," she said.

"My place is here," Kiro said, drawing himself upright. "With Nahj gone, and Halle . . . they need leaders." He lowered his eyes. "I know how you feel, princess. You think it's cowardly not to fight."

"There's more than one way to fight the Empire," Luke assured him.

"Luke's right," Leia agreed. "You can do plenty of good here. And I'll do everything I can to help."

"I know." Kiro pressed his hands to his face. "I'd like to be alone now, please."

"We should go, anyway," Leia said. "It's time for us to leave this place."

Far past time. But a part of her wished she could stay.

Ferus waited for Leia at the spaceport, needing to say goodbye. As soon as she spotted him, she sent Luke off to help Han and Elad with some final repairs, then greeted him warmly. Ever since the rescue, it was as if she'd been trying to make up for the way she'd treated him in the past. Ferus wished that he could enjoy it, finally having her respect after all these years. But he knew it wouldn't last. Not when she heard what he had to say.

"I've been thinking about your offer," Fess said. After thanking him for his part in the rescue, Leia had urged him to throw in his lot with the Rebellion. "I'm afraid I can't join your fight."

"If it's because of the way I've treated you—" Leia smiled ruefully. "Seems like I'm doing a lot of apologizing today. One more can't hurt."

"You've treated me as I deserved," Ferus said.

"I'm beginning to suspect you're not the man I thought you were, Fess. The Rebellion needs all the help it can get—you should join us."

Ferus wanted to. And not just because he missed the days when he could protect her at every turn.

He had turned it over and over in his mind. Obi-Wan had been no help. *Search inside yourself,* he had said. *Know the answer, you do.*

Even in his frustration, Ferus had smiled, remembering better days when he and the other Padawans had made a game of imitating Jedi Master Yoda's odd speech patterns. And, frustrated or not, Ferus had followed the older man's advice.

For whatever reason, Vader had taken a special interest in Leia. If he learned about his connection to the princess, or to Luke, nothing would stop him until they were both destroyed.

Or worse, Ferus thought. *Until he reclaims his children.*

Luke wasn't ready to be trained as a Jedi yet. He needed to grow stronger on his own before he learned how to access such great power. And Leia . . . Ferus suspected Leia was strong enough. But training her in the

Jedi ways would only make her more of a target. The stronger she grew, the greater the chance that Vader would sense the Force within her.

Just as he would sense Ferus, if Ferus stayed by her side.

Ferus had been watching and waiting for a long time. He had a new job now: Finding out what Darth Vader was up to.

And stopping him.

But how could he explain any of that to Leia?

"I don't put much faith in groups," he told her instead. "Eventually someone you trust will betray you."

She laughed bitterly. "You sound like Han. Afraid to believe in anything."

"I can't speak to whether Captain Solo is afraid, but I can assure you, *I'm* not."

Is that true? he wondered. *Or do I still fear repeating the mistakes of my past?* It felt like he was finally taking action, but was he just running away?

He missed the certainty of his youth with the Jedi, that rock solid knowledge that his choices were right. He saw it now in Luke.

Of course, he'd seen it in Anakin, too.

"I support the Rebellion, but I have other priorities right now," he said.

"What could be more important?" she asked angrily.

"You'd be surprised."

"Then go," she spit out. "Don't let me stop you."

"There are other ways to fight the Empire," Ferus pointed out. "I'm told that Kiro Chen —"

"Kiro's choice is not based on cowardice," she snapped. "Yours is."

Ferus told himself she was wrong. "I can't ask you not to be angry with me."

She crossed her arms. "I don't care enough to be angry."

"I can only ask that you trust me. This is the right thing." If it wasn't, if he left her alone and something happened . . .

He'd forgiven himself so much, but there would be no forgiveness for letting Leia die.

"You should go," she said harshly. "Minister Manaa is meeting me here, and then I'm getting off this planet. The Alliance needs me."

"One more thing, Leia," he said. This was probably a mistake, he knew that. But he couldn't help himself. She was the closest thing he had to a daughter — and she didn't know him at all. "Ferus."

"What's that supposed to mean?"

"It's my name," he said. "My real name. You know me as Fess Ilee, but that's a lie. I am Ferus Olin."

And for the first time in a long time, he was.

Even with her eyes closed, she can tell her father is standing in her doorway.

"I'm sorry I ran away," she says, opening her eyes. There is no point in pretending to be asleep. "Am I punished?"

"We'll talk about that in the morning." He kisses her forehead. "I'm just glad Fess brought you home to me."

When she hears his name, she gets angry all over again. "He didn't have to," she complains. "I'm no baby. I didn't need his help."

"But someday you may," her father says. "And I want you to remember this night. Fess will always be there when you need him. If anything ever happens to me —"

She giggles. Not because it's funny, but because maybe if she laughs, she won't be afraid. "Nothing's going to happen to you. Don't be stupid."

"If it does, and you're in trouble, go to Fess. He'll know what to do. He'll always take care of you."

Leia shook off the memory. She had believed almost everything her father had ever told her. But she'd never believed that. Fess, Ferus, whoever he was — obviously he wasn't the man Bail Organa had believed him to be. He wasn't anyone Leia could count on. It shouldn't have come as a surprise. It certainly shouldn't have mattered.

So why did she feel like she'd lost her father all over again?

CHAPTER TWENTY ONE

Everything always comes down to politics, Han thought in disgust, drawing in a deep breath of the stale air. He knew Leia was in her element, convincing the Prime Minister to do exactly as she wanted. But Han couldn't stand to sit around and watch. Making nice with chuff-sucking leeches — especially ones who'd sold you out to the Empire — just wasn't his thing.

Han wandered slowly through the streets around the spaceport, enjoying the breeze while he could. The air back on Yavin 4 was almost always heavy and still. Sometimes days would go by without a single breath of wind.

Then why am I going back? Just to drop them off, he told himself. *Then I'll get on my way.*

Sometimes Han thought it would just be easier to give in. Join the Rebels. Throw on a uniform. Fight the good fight.

But something always stopped him. He could join the Alliance, sure. But he'd be pretending to be someone he wasn't. Wearing a mask.

And he didn't like masks any more than he liked uniforms.

"Captain Solo!" A scrawny arm popped up out of the crowd, waving furiously. A moment later, Mazi's pale face appeared. The boy rushed toward him, his brothers close behind. "Didn't think we'd see you before we left."

"Going somewhere?" Han asked, surprised by how pleased he was to see the boys again. "And since when do you call me 'captain'?"

The brothers struck a military pose, arching their backs and saluting. "We're going to be respectful now," Jez said proudly.

Lan elbowed him in the side. "It's *respectable*," he said, rolling his eyes.

"We're got respect for him, that's *respectful*," Jez argued. "Full of respect. Get it?"

Lan smirked. "Full of respect — so that's like, the opposite of what I got for you. Respect*less*."

Mazi stepped in and caught Jez's arm just as he threw the punch. "We're going to be *respectful* to people like Captain Solo here — and that'll make us respectable, so people give us all their respect," he ordered them. He turned back to Han, his face flushed. "That's what the guy said, anyway."

"What guy?" Han asked.

"The guy who told us about the Rebellion," Mazi said eagerly. "We're going to be Rebels now. Fight back. We're shipping out tonight."

Han raised his eyebrows. Leia had designated several of the refugee leaders to act as recruiters in her stead. Apparently they were hard at work already. "Aren't you a little young?"

Identical scowls drooped across the brothers' faces. "No such thing as too young to stand up for what's right," Mazi said fiercely.

"The 'guy' tell you that, too?" Han asked.

Mazi shook his head. "That's all me."

"What gives, Captain Solo?" Lan asked. "Mazi said you'd be impressed."

"Yeah. Sure. I just meant . . ." He stopped, unsure of exactly what it was he did mean.

Han liked his life. No ties, no obligations, that's what he always said. He and Chewie were totally free. It was the only option for a man like him.

But Mazi wasn't a man yet. He had a choice.

"I just meant I can't believe anyone's going to trust you with a blaster," Han said lightly. "Try not to shoot yourself in the foot."

"At least we'll be able to see our target without electrobinoculars, old man," Mazi teased. "I'm surprised a guy with your ancient eyes and creaky bones can even *find* your blaster. Much less remember how to use it."

Han narrowed his eyes. "You better hope I'm too old to catch up with you," he warned.

The boys looked at each other in confusion.

"That's your cue to run," Han teased, balling his hands into fists. "Unless you want to see what these creaky old bones can still do . . ."

The boys burst into laughter, and took off running down the street. "See you soon, Captain!" Mazi shouted, as he disappeared into the crowds. "Don't forget us!"

"I won't," Han said quietly.

But he was alone again.

"Minister Manaa," Leia said coolly, as the Delayan leader joined her at the *Millennium Falcon*. He had invited her to his office, but she felt safer on her own turf. There was always the chance he could turn on her like his deputy had — but if he did, he'd get an unpleasant surprise. Luke and Elad were carefully hidden, blasters at the ready, poised to fire at the first sign of trouble. The setup had been Luke's idea, but Elad had quickly agreed. It was sweet, Leia thought, the way Elad stayed so close by Luke's side, especially recently. It was as if he saw something of himself in Luke, and felt a special need to encourage and protect him.

No wonder: They weren't that different. Two fighters, willing to sacrifice themselves if need be.

Unlike Ferus.

She forced down her anger. This meeting mattered — Ferus didn't.

"Princess Leia," the Prime Minister said. "Always an honor."

She waited.

"So glad to see you've emerged safely from your ordeal," he said, giving her a goofy, hopeful grin. "The people of Delaya care deeply for your well-being."

"So I've seen," Leia said dryly.

"And, of course, I can only offer my deepest apologies for the behavior of Deputy Minister Lyonn."

Leia raised her eyebrows. "Perhaps I should offer you *my* deepest apologies. After all the trouble you went to, trading me to the Empire, it seems rather rude of me to have escaped."

Manaa twisted his face into an unconvincing mask of horror. "Surely you're not suggesting *I* had something to do with Lyonn's despicable plans? Delaya has always been a great friend to the Alderaan people!"

"So that's why you've shut them up in those filthy warehouses with barely enough food or water to last out the week?" Leia snapped.

The warmth drained out of Manaa's smile. "I've done everything I can for the refugees. But my first responsibility is to my own people."

"As my responsibility is to mine." Leia glared at him until he looked away. "Which is why you wanted me out of the way."

He met her gaze again, his eyes steely. The good-natured fool was gone. "You'll never prove it," he said coolly. "And even if you could, what good would it do? Imperial reinforcements are on the way. If I were you, I'd take my ship away — and never come back."

He was right. He'd broken no laws; she had no power here.

"Look around you, Your Highness," he added, gesturing to the smoggy air, the streets crowded with factories. The city was as ugly as Alderaan had been beautiful. "Delaya has long paid for Alderaan's success. I see no reason why we should now pay for its failures."

"If I were you, Minister, I would give the Alderaan refugees the refuge they've been promised. Food, bacta, clothing." She ticked the items off on her fingers. "There are those who will help fund the effort — on my say-so. But that money is to go to the survivors. *Not* to the Delayan treasury."

"I don't see how you're in any position to give me orders," Manaa said, distaste in his voice.

"True," Leia admitted. "I'm an enemy of the Empire. As everyone who helps me is an enemy of the Empire."

"Exactly."

Leia felt like a krayt dragon toying with a woolamander. She hated this. But it was necessary.

"I can't imagine the Empire would take very kindly to your helping me," Leia said. "Much less collaborating with the Rebel Alliance."

"I haven't!" Manaa exclaimed. "I wouldn't!"

"And I'm sure Darth Vader will be very interested in your denials, especially once he receives anonymous reports of all your activities in support of the Rebels."

The blood had all drained from his face. "You wouldn't," he whispered.

"I'm sure Vader wouldn't blame innocent Delayans for the actions of its leader, but then . . ." Leia's chest tightened so much she could barely force the words out. *Saying it out loud doesn't make it true*, she promised herself. "The Empire didn't hesitate to fault the people of Alderaan for my actions, did they? I brought down their wrath on my planet . . . What makes you think I couldn't do the same to yours?"

Manaa's breath exploded from him in a miserable sigh. He sagged like a broken-down droid.

She was disgusted with herself. But she'd won.

"What do you want?" he asked, sounding defeated.

Leia told him.

"Well, it's done." Leia settled into the co-pilot's seat with a sigh. Chewbacca was down below, tinkering with the hyperdrive; Luke and Elad were doing calisthenics in the main hold. She and Han were alone in the cockpit.

"You made a *deal*?" Han asked incredulously.

"That was the idea," Leia said.

"I know, I just can't believe you're letting that dung grubber get away with it."

"Sometimes you have to make compromises," Leia told him.

"*I* don't have to do anything," Han pointed out. "Someone tries to get me, you better be sure I get *them*."

"*Some* of us try to take a longer view," Leia said. "We care about more than just the next payday."

"And some of us don't have a royal treasury to play with," Han retorted. "Or did you think I carted people like you across the galaxy for the fun of it?"

"I think you do it because you want to. Only reason you do anything," Leia said angrily. "Whatever you want, whenever you want. You're like a spoiled child."

"Hey, hold on there. If anyone here's spoiled, it's you."

"*Me*?"

"Yeah, you, sweetheart," he snarled. "You expect me to junk my whole life, just on your say-so? *Spoiled*."

"I don't expect anything from you but aggravation. You're just like *him*."

Han was lost. "Him who?"

"No one!"

Han never understood how they always ended up arguing — but usually he at least understood what they were arguing *about*. Not this time.

"How you live your life is your business," she said, ice cold. "You can't commit to anyone but yourself? *Fine.* But don't think you'll get my respect."

"Where's all this coming from, Highness?"

She exploded. "Stop calling me that!"

Apologize, he told himself. *It doesn't matter that you didn't do anything. Just apologize.*

"You want me to stop calling you that?" He smirked. "Then how 'bout you stop sitting up there on your throne and judging us peasants?"

"I don't have a throne anymore," she said in a rough voice. "The Empire *blew it up.*"

That stopped him.

He'd always thought of their arguments as an exchange of friendly fire. They fought the way children fight, backing off before drawing blood. Most of the time, he only said the things he did to get a rise out of her. He'd always assumed she felt the same way.

But this was different. There was true anger in her eyes. Like she meant every word.

"I fight for something greater than myself," she said. "So does Luke. Elad. But you? Nothing's greater than the great Han Solo, right? You don't care what the Empire does, if it doesn't directly affect you. Who knows if you care about anything."

"Don't tell me how I feel," he growled.

"Do you feel?" She laughed harshly. "In that case, I guess I'm wrong, you're not heartless. There's only one other reason for you to behave like you do. You're a coward."

Han slammed his fist down. "That's what you think, princess?"

"That's what I think, *captain*."

He stood up, fearing that if he stayed any longer, whatever was between them could break beyond repair. "I don't know who you're really mad at, princess, but it's not me. Deal with it, don't deal with it, I don't care. But leave me out of it."

He stormed out.

It made a good exit line, there was just one problem: He wasn't sure he believed it. Sure, maybe she was picking a fight to make herself feel better. Or maybe she was just telling him what she really thought of him.

Maybe she was right.

-7 was a patient man. Impatience was for those who had an ever-growing collection of needs. They rushed from one thing to another, always in motion, never satisfied. But X-7 had only one need: pleasing the Commander. He found it easy to remain still. To wait.

It was a useful skill for a hunter to possess.

But by the time the *Millennium Falcon* took off, X-7 was as close to impatient as he ever got. His prey was in sight, and he was like a coiled sand snake, ready to strike.

The Delayan communication system couldn't be trusted, especially with Vader's forces approaching the sector. X-7 forced himself to wait until he had returned to the ship. Then he forced himself to wait until he could slip away without anyone noticing. He sat patiently as Luke and Han bickered, as the protocol droid chattered and the Wookiee roared, as Han and Leia maneuvered around each other with icy politeness that barely masked their anger.

He waited until he got the privacy he required, and then he opened a secure channel to the Imperial Center and delivered news of his success.

"There is no doubt?" the Commander asked, barely disguising his eagerness.

"No doubt. The boy flies like no human I've ever seen," X-7 said, transferring his recording as they said. "He was up to the task, I'm sure of it. And it's the only explanation for why the princess allowed a young, untrained recruit from the edge of the galaxy into her inner circle. Nor could she have lied under the influence of the serum. *Luke Skywalker* destroyed the Death Star."

"Then he must die," the Commander said. "And soon, especially if the Dark One is on the hunt."

"As you wish."

"Do it however you'd like," the Commander said. "But make sure you shift the blame to someone else. After the kill, you'll stay with the Rebels and continue reporting on their activities."

"Consider it done."

The day, like most days on Yavin 4, had been unbearably hot. But as the sun set, a cool breeze cut through the humid air. Chucklucks buzzed and twittered from the Massassi trees, and bellybirds swooped overhead, slicing through the golden sunset. On nights like this, it wasn't uncommon for some of the younger recruits to strike up a game of smashball in one of the clearings.

It also wasn't uncommon for Luke to take a swoop bike ride through the jungle, glorying in the wind on his face and the world rushing by. It reminded him of his days racing across the dunes on Tatooine — the only moments in his childhood when he'd truly been happy. As if, pushing the swoop fast enough, he could outrun his life.

X-7 knew this, because Luke had confided in him. They were, after all, friends.

X-7 knew many things.

He knew which swoop Luke preferred to use.

He knew where on Yavin 4 a person could find ample quantities of explosive detonite charges.

He knew how to access Han Solo's bunk, and where its hiding places were. He knew where, for example, a person could hide ample quantities of detonite. Hide them precisely enough that Han would never suspect they were there — but that a cursory search of the bunk would quickly reveal them.

X-7 also knew how to rewire the ignition on a swoop bike, connecting it to the small packets of detonite tucked safely into the repulsorlift engines and the engine intake valve.

"Going out for a ride?" he asked, as Luke passed by. X-7 had positioned himself far enough from the swoop to avoid any shrapnel; close enough that he would be able to watch.

Luke grinned sheepishly. "You know I can't resist weather like this."

"I know," X-7 said. "It should be a memorable ride."

"Let's hope so," Luke said, hopping onto the swoop and waving goodbye.

Consider it done, X-7 had told the Commander, and he meant this literally. He had served the Commander for more than ten years, and never once had he failed to accomplish his mission. Once the order was given, its result was inevitable.

Luke Skywalker didn't know it yet, but he was already dead.